He'd made Gina suspicious.

And he didn't want her suspicious. He wanted her to treat him as she had before. As a friend. He wanted her to talk to him as if she liked him, Nick Balfour, the man. Not Nick Balfour, the eminent surgeon, or Nick Balfour, the very wealthy owner of the monstrous trust fund his grandfather had left him. Being valued for himself was an intoxicating experience that he didn't want to give up until he had to. He wanted to bask in the feeling for just a while longer.

He knew things would change once he told Gina the truth....

Dear Reader,

Spring is here. And what better way to enjoy nature's renewed vigor than with an afternoon on the porch swing, lost in four brand-new stories of love everlasting from Silhouette Romance?

New York Times bestselling author Diana Palmer leads our lineup this month with *Cattleman's Pride* (#1718), the latest in her LONG, TALL TEXANS miniseries. Get to know the stubborn, seductive rancher and the shy innocent woman who yearns for him. Will her love be enough to corral his heart?

When a single, soon-to-be mom hires a matchmaker to find her a practical husband, she makes it clear she doesn't want a man who inspires reckless passion…but then she meets her new boss! In Myrna Mackenzie's miniseries THE BRIDES OF RED ROSE classic legends take on a whole new interpretation. Don't miss *Midas's Bride* (#1719)!

Her Millionaire Marine (#1720), from *USA TODAY* bestselling author Cathie Linz, and part of her MEN OF HONOR miniseries, finds a beautiful lawyer making sure the marine she secretly adores fulfills his grandfather's will. Falling in love with the daredevil is *not* part of the plan!

And Judith McWilliams's *Dr. Charming* (#1721) puts a stranded female traveler in the path of a mysterious doctor; she agrees to take a job in exchange for a temporary home—with him. Now, this man makes her want to explore passion, but can he tempt her to take the *ultimate* risk?

Sincerely,

Mavis C. Allen
Associate Senior Editor

Please address questions and book requests to:
Silhouette Reader Service
U.S.: 3010 Walden Ave., P.O. Box 1325, Buffalo, NY 14269
Canadian: P.O. Box 609, Fort Erie, Ont. L2A 5X3

Dr. Charming

JUDITH McWILLIAMS

SILHOUETTE *Romance*®

Published by Silhouette Books

America's Publisher of Contemporary Romance

To Moses, with love and gratitude
for eight wonderful years

 SILHOUETTE BOOKS

ISBN 0-373-19721-7

DR. CHARMING

Visit Silhouette Books at www.eHarlequin.com

Printed in U.S.A.

Books by Judith McWilliams

JUDITH McWILLIAMS

began to enjoy romances while in search of the proverbial "happily-ever-after." But she always found herself rewriting the endings—and eventually the beginnings—of the books she read. Then her husband finally suggested that she write novels of her own, and she's been doing so ever since.

An ex-teacher with four children, Judith has traveled the country extensively with her husband and has been greatly influenced by those experiences. While not tending the garden or caring for her family, Judith does what she enjoys most—writing. She has also written under the name of Charlotte Hines.

Dear Diary,

I can't believe that all these years my mother had been lying about having so-called life-threatening ailments. As soon as I learned the truth, I got in a car and drove. I can finally have a life of my own.

So here I am stranded in beautiful New England. Did I mention my car was stolen and the most handsome man in the universe rescued me? I'm staying in his cabin temporarily. Now, wouldn't that scandalize Mother? Who knows what the future will bring…? I can't wait!

Footloose and fancy-free,

Gina

Prologue

"What do you think you're doing?"

Gina Tessereck mentally braced herself for the wave of guilt she always felt at upsetting her mother. To her surprise, it didn't come. Cautiously she probed and found nothing. Nothing at all. It was as if all of her feelings were locked behind a tightly closed door. A door she didn't dare open because if she did...

"I asked you a question, Gina! Why didn't you let me know you were home from work early? You know how much I worry at the least little unexplained noise. Really, at twenty-seven, you'd think you might have learned a little consideration. It won't be long before I'll be gone, and you can do exactly as you wish."

Gina looked up from the suitcase she had been haphazardly flinging clothes into, and studied her mother's small, delicate features. Why had she never noticed the hardness in her mother's china-blue eyes or the petulant droop of her mouth?

"What is the matter with you? Why are you standing

there gawking at me? You haven't lost your job, have you?" Helen's voice sharpened.

"I didn't lose it, Mother. I resigned it. Effective immediately."

Gina walked over to her closet and opened the door, instinctively rejecting the clothes inside. All those ruffles and soft pastels didn't suit her. They suited her mother's petite figure and blond coloring. On her own five-ten frame they looked fussy, and the pale pastels made her look washed-out.

Never again would she buy something that didn't suit her simply to keep the peace, she vowed as she closed the door with a decided snap.

"How many times have I told you not to slam doors?" her mother demanded.

"I don't know," Gina said honestly. "But I do know that this is the last time you'll ever have to do it, because I'm leaving."

"Leaving!" Her mother clutched her chest and started to gasp. "I feel…"

Gina watched with a feeling of numbness. "You missed your calling, Mother. You should have gone on the stage."

Turning away, Gina scooped the last of her underwear out of her dresser drawer, tossed it into her suitcase and yanked the zipper closed.

Her mother's mouth fell open in shock at Gina's totally unexpected response. "How can you say that to your own mother?"

"Come to that, how could you lie to your own daughter? Your doctor called me at work this morning and asked me to come by his office on my lunch hour. It was a most enlightening meeting." Gina cringed at the humiliating memory. "He gave me a lecture about how

I was stifling you. About how you'd told him I'd sabotaged your efforts to get a job to help fill your time since Dad died.'' Gina's rigid control cracked slightly at the thought of her beloved father. ''The doctor also assured me there was absolutely nothing wrong with your heart.''

''You probably misunderstood him,'' her mother insisted. ''You really aren't the world's brightest person, you know.''

Gina ignored the oft-repeated comment.

''And after I left his office, I got to wondering what else you might have lied to me about, so I went to see the lawyer who handled Dad's estate.''

''You had no right!''

Gina's light blue eyes momentarily darkened with anger. ''As one of the beneficiaries, I had every right. I found out that, far from leaving you almost penniless as you'd claimed, Dad left you more than enough money to live on. Not only that but he left me enough money to finish my degree.''

Gina jerked her suitcase off the bed and started toward the door.

''But you can't leave me!'' her mother screamed. ''I love you.''

Gina paused and looked back at her mother. ''Is love your excuse or your explanation for what you've done?''

Her mother ignored the question. ''Where are you going? What are you going to do?''

''I'm going as far away from here as I can get, and as for what I'm going to do, I intend to start living instead of just existing,'' Gina said as she turned and walked out the door.

Chapter One

Gina gently touched the brakes of her car as she rounded a sharp bend in the narrow Massachusetts road and saw the lights of a small village directly ahead.

She shifted restlessly, trying to relieve some of the stiffness driving all day had caused. Her stomach, as if in sympathy with her muscles, gave a sudden rumble, reminding her that it had been a long time since lunch.

When she reached the village, she slowed to a crawl, looking for someplace to eat. Finding a brightly lit diner, she parked in front of it.

Grabbing her purse, she got out of the car and automatically locked it. A fugitive gust of crisp September wind raised goose bumps on her bare arms and whipped her reddish-brown hair into her face. She absently pushed it back as she considered unlocking the car and digging through her luggage to find a sweater. Finally she decided she wouldn't be outside long enough for it to be worth the trouble.

She started toward the restaurant and then paused

when a garish sign across the street advertising Bill's Bar caught her eye. Turning, she studied the faintly dilapidated building, taking in what seemed to be a score of neon signs advertising beers, most of which she'd never heard of.

Her gaze swung back to the restaurant. It looked staidly middle class and boringly respectable. Whereas Bill's Bar looked daring. Adventurous. In keeping with the new life she was determined to carve for herself.

Definitely Bill's Bar, she decided.

Not giving herself a chance to change her mind, she quickly crossed the street, pushed open the bar's door and stepped inside.

Nervously her gaze swept the crowded, noisy room. Feeling conspicuous, she hurriedly sat down at an empty table near the door. Picking up the cardboard menu lying on the red-and-white-checked plastic tablecloth, she studied it. It was heavy on imported beers and light on food.

A middle-aged waitress appeared a few minutes later. "What can I get you?"

"A bowl of chili, apple pie and a cup of coffee," Gina said.

"Won't be a minute." The waitress headed back to the kitchen, calling out Gina's order to someone named Margie as she went.

Gina leaned against the back of the scuffed wooden chair and surreptitiously studied the bar's patrons while she waited for her food. A large party at the back seemed to be having a great time. A wistful smile curved Gina's mouth at the infectious sound of their laughter.

"Here you are, miss." The waitress slapped a big bowl filled to the brim with chili down in front of her.

A steaming cup of coffee followed. ''I'll get your pie in a minute.''

Gina was adding milk to her coffee when the bar's door opened and a slither of chilly night air wrapped itself around her ankles.

''Hey, Nick, how's the arm coming?'' a man from the back of the room called out.

Curious, Gina turned to see who Nick was. Her eyes widened when she saw the man standing just inside the door. He was tall. At least six inches taller than she was. And broad. She measured the substantial width of his shoulders beneath the thick, cream Aryan sweater he was wearing.

Unconsciously her tongue moistened her lower lip as her eyes traveled down over his flat stomach and his long, jean-covered legs.

Hastily she glanced down at her chili, trying to stifle her sudden, inexplicable fascination with his body. She took a slow, deep breath, hoping the flush she could feel burning her face wasn't visible to anyone else in the room.

What was the matter with her? she wondered uneasily. So what if the man was built like the embodiment of every sexual fantasy she'd ever had. She was old enough to know that sexual attraction was nothing more than nature's way of ensuring the continuation of the species.

Compulsively her gaze returned to the man. Maybe so, she conceded, but in his case, nature had certainly baited one very attractive trap.

She watched from beneath her lashes as the man walked toward the bar, sat down and reached for a glass of beer the bartender placed in front of him without a word ever having been spoken.

A regular patron, Gina concluded as she studied the

man's ruggedly carved features, her eyes lingering on the strength of his square chin. He had a strong face. Not conventionally handsome, but arresting. Full of character and strength.

Gina watched as he awkwardly picked up his beer with his left hand. Curious, her gaze swung to his right hand and she noticed a cast peeping out from beneath the sleeve of his sweater. He appeared to have broken either his arm or his wrist.

Her eyes narrowed speculatively as he impatiently shoved his fingers through his inky black hair. Nick, whoever he was, did not appear to be in the best of humors. Was his arm painful? she wondered, finding the idea strangely unacceptable. Or maybe something else was bothering him? Maybe he was recovering from a bad relationship? she thought fancifully. Maybe his heart was broken?

Gina's gaze traced over the sensual line of his lips and mentally jettisoned the idea. He looked like a man who would break hearts, not have his own broken.

Absently, she picked up her spoon and started to eat, her eyes never leaving Nick. He appealed to her on an instinctive level she hadn't even been aware had existed until now.

Sex, she mocked her own reaction. That was all it was. Plain old animal attraction.

But what an animal Nick was, she thought dreamily. The king of the beasts. Rugged and...

"Here's your pie, miss," the waitress's voice broke into her thoughts.

Gina blinked and looked down, surprised to see that she'd finished her chili.

"Thank you," Gina said, hoping the woman hadn't noticed her preoccupation with Nick.

It was a vain hope. The waitress leaned closer and whispered, ''That's our Nick Balfour. He has a place outside-a town. Known him since he was a kid. And his folks before him. And he ain't got no wife tucked away like some I could mention. You like what you see, kiddo, grab it. Life's too short not to.''

Gina's stomach did a sudden flip-flop, and her fingers began to tingle as she imagined what Nick would feel like if she were brave enough to take the woman's advice and grab him. He'd feel firm and warm and…

''Think about it, kiddo. Like they say, you only go round once.''

''Um, thank you,'' Gina muttered.

Satisfied, the waitress gave her a thumbs-up and sauntered off.

Taking a deep breath to slow her racing heart, Gina looked back at Nick. He was staring into his beer as if he expected to find the secret of eternal life written on the bottom of the glass.

There was no getting around it. She found Nick Balfour fascinating, she faced the fact with her usual lack of self-deception. At least, she found his physical appearance fascinating, and she'd very much like to find out if his personality measured up to his body's promise.

No, nobody could have a personality as great as his body was, she conceded. She simply wanted to see if the personality came anywhere close.

So how did one go about picking up a man in a bar? Gina searched her memory for a clue and came up blank. The situation had never come up before.

Think. She tried to organize her muddled thoughts into a plan. Women have been picking up men since time immemorial. If they can do it, so can you.

Maybe she could make a comment that demanded an

answer? Something like what's a gorgeous hunk like you doing nursing a beer in a backwater bar like this? Gina choked on her coffee at the thought of actually being blasé enough to say something that trite.

There was always the weather or that old chestnut about haven't we met before. But even if she was willing to try such a clichéd opening, first she had to get close enough to him to do it.

She laid her fork down beside the now-empty pie plate and considered the problem. If she walked over to him and tried to strike up a conversation, and he brushed her off or, even worse, ignored her, she'd be mortified.

But did it really matter if she was embarrassed? She didn't know any of these people. Did she really care what they thought? No, she didn't, but she did care what Nick thought, she conceded. It might not make any sense, considering the fact that he was a stranger, but she did care what he thought of her.

She cast a furtive glance at his uncompromising profile. He was still staring into his beer. He certainly wasn't watching her. She doubted if he'd even seen her when he'd come in. Not *really* seen her. Men almost never did. She was too tall and too skinny and too…too nondescript to generate much interest in the opposite sex.

Face it, Gina Tessereck, she told herself. You haven't got what it takes to set masculine hearts ablaze. But it would be nice if she could ignite a spark of interest in just one, she thought wistfully.

She grimaced. The list of what she would like to be different in her life was as long as her arm, and moaning about it wasn't going to change anything. Only action would change things. And no matter how uncomfortable or embarrassing it might turn out to be, she was determined to change. To grow. She'd given herself until the winter semester at college began to expand her horizons. And she intended to start by traveling and by exploring an emotional relationship with a man.

Compulsively, her gaze returned to Nick. He looked as if he were positively bursting with fantastic possibilities. All she had to do was to have the courage to tap them. Her lips firmed in determination.

Opening her purse, she took out money to pay her bill and dropped it on the table along with a good-size tip for the helpful waitress as she mulled over the problem of making contact with Nick.

She could walk up to the bar and ask the bartender for a bottle of beer to take out with her, she considered. Then, while the bartender was getting it, she could turn to Nick and ask him if he knew of any bed-and-breakfast places nearby. It was a reasonable question to use to start a conversation.

Swallowing nervously, Gina got to her feet. But before she could move toward the bar, someone touched her arm.

Startled, she turned to find herself looking at a slightly overweight, middle-aged man who gave her a leering smile and then ran his eyes over her body with a lascivious look that made her skin crawl.

"I beg your pardon!" Gina gave him her best imitation of her mother's freezing outrage. "I don't believe I've met you."

"That's easy enough to fix. I'm Jim, and who are you, babycakes?"

Gina blinked uncertainly, not sure what to do. Jim wasn't following the script. He was supposed to retreat in the face of her obvious disinterest. Instead he'd inched closer. Close enough for her to smell the sickly sweet odor of his cologne. Her stomach rolled protestingly.

"I'm not interested," she muttered, not wanting him near her, but also not wanting to bolt for the door and give up any chance of speaking to Nick Balfour.

"How do you know that? Why don't you let me buy you a beer, and we can get acquainted?" Jim insisted, seeming to find her nervousness a turn-on.

Nick turned as the whiny pitch of Jim's voice grated across his nerves. His eyes narrowed speculatively as he saw the woman the older man was trying to pick up. Jim's taste in women had definitely improved. Not only was she satisfyingly tall, but... His eyes slipped down the length of her slender figure, lingering on the slight thrust of her breasts beneath her dark-green shirt.

He shivered as he imagined the feel of her breast filling his hand. Trying to control his body's instinctive response to the provocative thought, he forced his gaze upward, only to find that her face was just as intriguing as her body. He studied the slight tilt of her nose with its faint dusting of freckles, which perfectly matched her reddish-brown hair, before moving on to the full curve of her pink lips. They made him long to feel them beneath his own. To find out if they really were as soft and pliable as they looked.

He watched as her face paled in annoyance at Jim's refusal to take no for an answer. Or was it fear?

Odd, he thought curiously. A woman that attractive should be experienced enough to flatten lechers like Jim without even thinking about it. And yet she didn't seem to be able to shake him off.

Why not? he wondered, and then hastily quashed his interest. It wasn't any of his business, he told himself. He couldn't afford to get involved. Women, especially those who looked the way she did, demanded more from a man than he had to give. Bitter experience had taught him that.

Nick sighed as he saw the sudden flare of panic in her expressive eyes when Jim inched even closer to her. She shouldn't be out alone if she didn't know how to deal with the Jims of the world. She had no right involving innocent bystanders in her problems.

But right or not, he was unable to resist the growing fear he could see in her face. It wouldn't take long, he told himself as he got off the bar stool. He'd slap down Jim, walk her to her car and that would be the end of it. He refused to even acknowledge the flash of loss he felt at the thought.

"You heard the lady, Jim." A dark, velvety voice flowed soothingly over Gina's agitated nerves. She turned to find herself staring into Nick Balfour's cool gray eyes. She felt as if she could drown in their incredible depths. She took a deep breath, trying to break their mesmerizing hold on her, and the faintly spicy fragrance of his cologne filled her nostrils.

"Give it up, Jim." Nick's voice hardened perceptibly when Jim didn't move.

"Hey, no call to get all bent outta shape, Nick." Jim held up his hands as if warding him off. "I didn't realize I was poaching. But if you should decide you want a change, babycakes, give me a call. Everyone knows me."

Gina's breath escaped on a relieved sigh as Jim returned to his own table.

"I'm Nick Balfour. I'll walk you to your car."

"Gina Tessereck, and thank you," she muttered as she scrambled for something bright and witty to say.

Something that would make him want to linger to get to know her better.

"Do you come here often?" Gina mentally cringed as she heard the inane question emerge from her mouth.

"No. Where are you parked?" he asked her as they emerged from the bar.

"Across the street," she said, trying not to let her chagrin at his clear disinterest show.

His hand unexpectedly closed around her arm as she stepped off the curb, and he jerked her back as a car hurtled past them.

Gina landed against his chest. She could feel the scratchy sensation of his wool sweater against her cheek, and the heat pouring from his large body momentarily suspended her rational thought.

"You okay?" he asked when she didn't move.

No, she wasn't okay, she thought frantically. She was fast losing her entire sense of perspective, and she didn't have a clue as to what to do about it.

"Did that fool Jim really upset you that much?" Nick asked, and Gina felt her stomach twist at his concerned tone.

"No, I...I..." I always sound like the village idiot around sexy men, she thought in dismay.

"Are you well enough to drive?"

Gina took a deep breath and forced herself to step away from him.

"I'm fine," she blurted out, and then could have screamed in frustration when she realized that she'd just blown a great chance. If she'd claimed to have been too upset to drive, he might have offered to buy her a coffee while she calmed down.

"Is that blue Ford yours?" He pointed to a car parked a little down from the restaurant.

"No." Gina shook her head. "I have a brown Camry. It's parked…" She broke off as she realized that her car wasn't where she'd left it.

Frowning, she looked up and down the street. She was positive she'd parked in front of the restaurant. She turned and checked the other side of the street. There were no Toyotas of any make.

"I don't understand," she said. "I left my car right there."

Nick watched as she pointed to the vacant spot behind the Ford, momentarily distracted by her slender fingers with their shortly cut, clear-varnished nails. He hated long, luridly colored nails.

"I know I left it there," she repeated as if the very strength of her words could make her car reappear.

"Either you're mistaken about where you left it or someone took it." Nick stated the obvious.

"Thank you, Sherlock Holmes!" she snapped, fear and frustration swamping her awe of him.

"Everybody hates the messenger!" Nick gave a long-suffering sigh.

"Sorry, I didn't mean to snap," she muttered. "But everything I own is in that car. It can't have been stolen. I mean, this is rural Massachusetts, for heaven's sake!"

"You think big cities have a monopoly on crime?" he asked dryly when he really wanted to ask why she was traveling around the countryside with everything she owned. Didn't she have a home? And a man who cared enough to keep her there?

"I know crime is everywhere," she said. "But knowing it's out there doesn't mean I expected it to find me. I was only gone long enough to eat dinner. And I locked it." Her voice rose despairingly.

Nick's experienced ear caught the first sign of hysteria in her voice, and he hastily moved to head it off.

"You'll need to report it." He gave her a simple task to handle.

"To whom?" Gina looked vaguely around the deserted street as if she expected a policeman to materialize out of the pavement.

"Amos Mygold is the sum total of our law enforcement. This time of night he's probably at home."

Gina swayed slightly as she suddenly remembered that all her traveler's checks were in the car's glove compartment.

Nick instinctively reached for her, steadying her against his chest.

The feel of his hard body pressing against her from thigh to chest held her growing panic at bay. This close to him, she found it impossible to focus on anything as mundane as being stranded in a strange town, filled with even stranger inhabitants—if Jim was any sample—with very little money.

"It isn't that bad." Nick's deep voice flowed comfortingly over her.

"That's what you think," she muttered into the thick wool of his sweater. "All my traveler's checks were in the car."

"All of them?"

"Yes." Gina forced herself to step out of the comfort of his arms. She was a competent adult, she reminded herself. She could handle this. "I didn't want to risk losing them if someone snatched my purse."

"Well, that part of your plan worked," he said dryly, and Gina gave a muffled gurgle of laughter.

Nick felt a flare of interest at the intriguing sound. She was such an odd combination. Her appearance suggested a poised, sophisticated woman, but her reactions seemed much more vulnerable. He found the combination fascinating.

"You can get the traveler's checks reissued," he said. "All you need to do is call the company with the serial numbers…" He stopped at her pained expression.

"You do have the serial numbers, don't you?"

"Of course I do. I even separated them from the checks the way the bank said to. It's just that I put the numbers in my suitcase in case someone stole my purse."

"Where do you live that you're always worried about your purse being stolen?" Nick asked.

"At the moment in my car," she said with a despairing look at the empty space where it had been parked.

"Which means you are now homeless," he said, regretting the words the minute he saw her face pale.

"Quite." Gina straightened her spine and tried to sound more purposeful than she felt. She'd wanted to stand on her own two feet, and this was her chance. So why wasn't she feeling more elated at the opportunity?

"Your car is insured?"

"Oh, yes. I'll call the insurance company first thing in the morning." She tried not to think about where she was going to spend the night and how she was going to get there. Did towns this size have rental car offices? she wondered. At least she still had her credit card in her purse so she wasn't exactly penniless. And there was the legacy from her father. She'd call the lawyer who'd handled her father's estate first thing in the morning and ask him to wire some money to her.

"Is there anyone you want to call?" Nick probed.

"No," Gina said shortly, having no intention of telling him why. The story of her life to date made her sound like a fool. But then, maybe she was, she thought glumly. First her mother had used her love to manipulate her, and then some thief had stolen her car. She wasn't exactly batting a thousand.

Nick digested the uncompromising negative, wondering what she was running from. The frustrated pain in her voice certainly suggested something.

"It's going to take a while for you to get things straightened out," Nick said slowly as an idea burst full-blown into his mind, the brilliance of it momentarily stunning him. "In the meantime, I think we could be of use to each other. You'll need a place to stay, and I could use a temporary housekeeper."

He gestured with his cast. "With my right hand out of commission, I can't do much, and what little I can do with my left, I do slowly and badly. Not only that, but I've had enough of Bill's chili to last me a lifetime. Being my temporary housekeeper would give you a place to stay until you sort things out, and would give me a clean house and a few meals," he said, hoping his explanation sounded credible.

He hadn't hired a housekeeper already because he hadn't wanted a stranger intruding on his privacy, but the thought of Gina sharing his house filled him with anticipation.

Gina swallowed against the sudden spurt of excitement that short-circuited her breathing. Surely he couldn't be offering her a job? At his house? Just the two of them? Alone together?

"Have you done any housekeeping?" he asked her.

"If you mean as a job, no. But I can certainly clean and cook," she said absently, her mind busily considering his unexpected offer.

She knew full well she should refuse. Prudence demanded it. She might be monstrously attracted to this man, but she didn't know him well enough to share a house with him.

But the people in the bar did. She remembered how someone in the back had greeted him by name and what the waitress had said about having known Nick all his life. If he had had any unsavory tendencies, surely his neighbors would know about them and react to him accordingly. Secrets were impossible to keep in a small town, weren't they?

Not only that, but his offer made a great deal of sense. They both had something the other needed. And it would be a wonderful chance to practice relating to a sexy man, she reminded herself.

Strangely enough, the fact that he really needed a housekeeper depressed her. It would have been nice to have thought that Nick was so attracted to her that he was creating the job as an excuse to keep her around. But just because he wasn't initially attracted to her didn't mean that she might not grow on him, she assured herself.

Gina felt a sudden flush warm her cheeks at the thought of where she'd like to grow on him. Dangerous, her common sense chided her. A man like Nick Balfour could destroy a woman's peace of mind. But what a way to go, her emotions countered.

"What kind of work do you do?" she asked in an attempt to find out a little more about him.

Nick frowned slightly. He didn't want to lie to her, but on the other hand, he didn't want to tell her the truth, either. Invariably, whenever he mentioned that he was a thoracic surgeon to an attractive woman, he got one of two reactions. Either they saw dollar signs and started sizing him up as a potential husband who could afford to indulge their tastes for luxury, or they launched into a recital of medical symptoms—either their own or someone else's.

He didn't want either of those reactions from Gina. He wanted her to see him as a man, without the accompanying baggage of his profession confusing the issue.

Gina watched as his face hardened into a reserved mask, wondering what had caused it. Her question? Had it embarrassed him? Could he have a humdrum, go-nowhere type of job and think she might look down on him because of it?

"I'm a technician," Nick finally said, remembering what one of his more acerbic professors had once said about surgeons. "And I have to have complete mobility in my right hand to work. So for the time being, I'm just marking time while my bone knits. Speaking of jobs, are you on vacation?" he slipped the question in.

"No, I was a data-entry clerk in Chicago. I got fed up with the same old routine and decided I wanted a change. I'd always wanted to see New England in the fall, so here I am," Gina said.

There was more to her leaving her job than that, Nick decided as he watched the shadows darken her eyes. Something or someone had hurt her very badly to send her running this far.

"Think of my offer as a chance to see the fall foliage up close and in depth." Nick carefully kept his voice casual. He didn't want to scare her off with too many questions. For some reason it was becoming increasingly important to him that she stay.

"But I don't really know you. You could be an ax murderer for all I know," she blurted.

"The sheriff will vouch for me," Nick countered.

"You can ask him for a character reference when we report your car stolen."

Uncertainly, Gina studied the calm, gray depths of his eyes, unsure of what to do. All her life she'd done what was expected of her. What was conventional. Maybe it was time to do what she wanted to. To follow her feelings where they led, and to hell with caution.

Gina took a deep breath and said, "Thank you. I'll take the job until I can get everything sorted out."

Chapter Two

"Well, that about covers it, Ms. Tessereck. I'll get on to the state police with a description of your car," said the rotund little man whom Nick had introduced as Chief Mygold.

"What do you think the chances are that they'll find it?" Gina asked him.

He sighed and ran his pudgy fingers over his balding head. "Depends," he finally said.

"On what?" she persisted, feeling as if she was pulling teeth.

"On who took it," he said. "If it was a couple of kids who took it to go joyriding, then they'll abandon it as soon as they're done, and you should have it back in a day or two. But this being a Friday night don't argue well for that scenario."

Nick looked from Gina's blank expression to the chief's mournful one and said, "Well, if she won't ask, I will. What does it being a Friday night have to do with anything?"

"The high school's football team is playing an away game," the chief said.

"And all the kids who might have pulled a stunt like that are at the game?" Gina deduced.

"Yep," Chief Mygold said.

"Which narrows the list of suspects down to whom?" Nick asked.

"Someone who stole it to convert to cash. All your stuff being in the back seat would have only made it that much more tempting. You should never leave things lying in a car in plain sight," the chief said.

"Sorry," she muttered, trying not to show her annoyance at his attitude that this was all her fault. First she wanted to get her car back, and then she'd tell him what she thought of his "blame the victim" policy.

"You should have left your stuff at home," the chief belabored the point.

"Ah, but I was running away from home," Gina said.

Nick's eyes narrowed at her words, wondering if she meant them literally. And if so, where was this home she was running from? Or was it a person she was escaping from? Like a lover or a husband?

His eyes dropped to her left hand. It was bare. Nor could he see any sign that she might have recently worn any rings. Not that it mattered to him personally, he assured himself. He had no intention of getting emotionally involved with her. He didn't dare. A personal relationship would demand more from him than he could give.

He was just going to take advantage of her being stranded to get his house cleaned and to get a few home-cooked meals. And to get some company. He felt a prickle of anticipation. It would be nice to have someone to talk to in the evenings.

"Now, then, Ms. Tessereck, how will I contact you if I hear anything?" Chief Mygold asked.

"She'll be at my place," Nick said. "She's going to be my temporary housekeeper."

"Um," Gina muttered uncertainly, with a quick glance at Nick's rugged features. "Sheriff, being a stranger in town...and while I appreciate Nick's offer, I mean..."

"You mean you want me to assure you that you won't wake up one morning to find yourself murdered in your bed?" Mygold broke into her convoluted sentence.

"Strictly speaking, being murdered precludes waking up," Nick observed.

"It precludes most everything," Gina said tartly, refusing to back down at the humor she could see in Nick's gorgeous eyes.

"Don't you worry about Nick here, Ms. Tessereck. I've known him, man and boy, and he ain't the type to force himself on a woman." Mygold gave a wheezy chuckle. "Beating the women off is closer to what he faces. Same as his father before him. Why I remember—"

"Spare the poor woman tales of my family tree." Nick hastily sidetracked the sheriff before he said something about him being a doctor. Or that his great-grandfather had been in business with George Eastman of Kodak fame.

Gina relaxed slightly at the chief's words. She'd been almost sure that Nick was as trustworthy as he looked, but it was nice to have her opinion vindicated. Nor did she particularly want to hear about Nick's prowess with women. She wasn't interested in the past, only the future.

"If I hear anything, I'll give you a ring at Nick's, Ms. Tessereck," Mygold said.

Gina nodded, not liking the sound of that "if."

"I'll check back with you in the morning," she said as Mygold walked them to the door. She was determined to make him understand that she wasn't going to be put off with vague promises.

"Tomorrow's Saturday," Mygold said cryptically as he closed the door behind them.

"What does tomorrow being Saturday have to do with anything?" Gina asked as she followed Nick down the front steps. "Does he only solve crimes during the week?"

"He doesn't solve crimes anytime," Nick said with what Gina thought was heartless cheerfulness. "If your car gets found, it'll be the state police who do it."

Gina grimaced, not feeling any better about having her suspicions about Mygold's incompetence confirmed. "If he can't solve crimes, then why is he the sheriff?" she asked in exasperation.

"Because he's the local undertaker." Nick unlocked the passenger door of his battered pickup. "You will note that I locked my door?"

"I did, too, for all the good it did me. Besides, who in his right mind would steal this…thing? They'd be afraid it would break down before they made their getaway."

"Don't malign the wheels that are providing your transportation. I've had Old Octavius since I was sixteen."

And he hadn't been able to afford to replace it yet? Gina wondered as she climbed onto the front seat, being careful to avoid the rip in the upholstery. If he was that short of cash, how could he afford to pay a housekeeper's salary? Even a temporary one like hers. But on the other hand, if he didn't have the money to pay for one, why had he offered her the job?

Could he have felt sorry for her? The appalling thought made her feel faintly ill. No! She refused to even consider the idea. She might not have much in the line of sex appeal for men, but neither had she ever noticed that they pitied her. Mostly they ignored her.

It was probably just as he'd said. He'd seen a chance to have someone take care of the household chores while his arm was in a cast, and he'd grabbed it.

She studied him in the dim light from the truck's dashboard, wondering exactly what he did for a living. He'd said he was a technician, but that could mean anything.

Her eyes lingered on his left hand where it gripped the steering wheel. His fingers were long and powerful-looking with neatly trimmed nails that were immaculately clean. There were no little cuts and scrapes that one would expect on a man who earned his living working with his hands. Although, since she had no idea how long it had been since he'd broken his arm, any abrasions could have healed. Maybe his employer had laid him off when he'd broken his arm. She had no idea what the labor laws regarding accidents were. That could be why he was so reticent about his work. He might be embarrassed about being unemployed.

Gina rubbed her forehead, which was beginning to ache from stress. It had been a long day even before the crowning finale of getting her car stolen.

"You okay?" Nick shot her a quick glance.

"Just confused. Tell me, why would being the undertaker make Mygold the sheriff?"

"Small town, not too many deaths, so he has the time. And he could use the extra money."

"Oh." Gina considered the words. "Isn't there a potential conflict of interest there?"

"Only if Mygold had a very Machiavellian turn of mind, and believe me, his mind only turns on his dinner and his bowling average. You must not be familiar with small towns?" Nick slipped the question in.

"No."

Nick waited, but she made no attempt to elaborate on the single word. Was it because she didn't want to talk about her past or because she was a naturally reticent woman? Just because he'd never run across one before didn't mean they didn't exist.

It figured, he thought in frustration. Usually he couldn't get a woman to shut up. But let him find one who promised to be interesting, and he couldn't get the first personal fact out of her.

"Where do you live?" Gina asked as they left the village behind.

"About a mile outside of town. It's a vacation cottage my great-grandfather built, and my parents gave it to me."

"Oh?" Gina let her voice rise questioningly. Nick Balfour sounded like an educated man. And he had excellent manners when he cared to use them. She flushed slightly as she remembered how he'd rescued her from that guy in the bar. He clearly hadn't wanted to be bothered, but he'd done it anyway.

But he also gave her the impression that he didn't suffer fools gladly. That attitude might not go over well in a work environment. Every office she'd worked in during the past four years had had at least one pompous fool in a position of authority, so it made sense that a factory would be the same. Had Nick run afoul of someone like that?

To her disappointment, Nick didn't add any facts, and Gina pressed her lips together to hold back the personal questions she wanted to ask. It's none of your business, she told herself. Just because she was intensely curious about him didn't mean she had any right to keep prying into something he obviously didn't want to talk about.

Gina jerked upright as she suddenly realized something.

"What's the matter?" Nick hastily scanned the road for suicidal wildlife.

"I haven't got any clothes," she blurted out.

Nick's fingers involuntarily tightened around the steering wheel as the most incredible image of Gina lying naked in his bed suddenly filled his mind. He took a deep breath, hastily banished the intoxicating image, and asked, "What do you mean?"

"Just what I said. I don't know why I didn't remember till now, but all my clothes were in the car. All I have is what I'm wearing. I haven't even got a nightgown."

And if there were anyplace around here open at this time of night, he'd turn around and buy her a nightgown himself, Nick thought. A satin one. A pale rose satin nightgown with ecru lace around a bodice cut low enough to offer tantalizing glimpses of her breasts. And a midthigh slit up the side so that he could catch glimpses of her long legs as she moved.

"Is there any place I could buy something to wear?" Gina asked with a hopeless look around the wooded area he was driving through.

"Nothing closer than Vinton, which is twenty miles away. Except for the convenience store, all the local shops are geared to the tourist trade, and they close at five. I'll take you to Vinton first thing tomorrow and buy you some clothes.''

''You can take me, but I'll buy my own,'' she said firmly. ''My credit card was in my purse so I still have it.''

''Consider it an advance on your salary,'' Nick said.

That certainly sounded as if he could afford to pay her, she thought. Or was it a case of him doing without something in order to come up with her salary? She instinctively rejected the idea.

''About this job...''

''You can't weasel out now,'' he said, suddenly afraid that she might have changed her mind.

''I'm not trying to 'weasel' out of anything! I was simply going to say that I would prefer a trade to a salary.''

''A trade?'' he asked cautiously.

''I'll do some housekeeping chores in exchange for room and board for a few days.''

Nick gritted his teeth in frustration. He hadn't even gotten her home yet, and she was already making plans to cut out as soon as she could. Where was she in such a hurry to get to? Or was it that she was in a hurry to get to someone?

He felt a sharp twist of some emotion that he refused to analyze.

''When I said temporary, I meant weeks, not days. Why don't you give the job a two-week try?'' he said. ''Unless someone's expecting you somewhere?''

''It's not that. I just don't want to tie myself down.'' In case he turned out to have zero interest in her as a person, she thought. In that case she sure didn't want to hang around and be constantly reminded of what she couldn't have.

''I would think your lack of transportation, to say nothing of lack of money, would do that more effectively than a job. A job gives you freedom to make choices. If you didn't like being a data-entry clerk, what does interest you?'' He decided the question wouldn't seem unreasonable from someone offering her a job.

''Teaching,'' she said promptly. ''I had almost three years of my teaching degree finished before I had to quit to help out at home when my father was diagnosed with lung cancer. He died thirteen months later. That was two and a half years ago.'' Her voice broke on the painful memories.

Nick reached across and gently brushed the tips of his fingers across her cheek in a gesture of sympathy that unexpectedly made her want to cry.

She took a deep breath to steady her voice and continued, ''He left me enough money to finish my degree. I'm enrolled at the University of Illinois for the winter semester, which starts in January. In the meantime I'm determined to do a Robert Frost.''

'''The road less traveled,''' Nick quoted, wondering why she hadn't used her father's legacy to go back to school immediately after his death instead of taking a job that by her own admission she'd hated. There was something else there that she didn't want to talk about. And for the moment he had no choice but to respect her silence.

''That's right.'' Gina blinked in surprise that he'd understood the reference. Not many people she knew were acquainted with Frost's work.

''How about if you try the job for two weeks?'' he offered.

Gina thought it over a moment and then said, ''All right. Two weeks.''

"And after that, we can negotiate a longer stay."

"I really am just passing through," Gina said, feeling she was warning herself as much as him.

"So pass through at a walk. That way you can get a good look at the scenery."

"From what I've seen so far, it's certainly worth looking at," Gina latched on to the impersonal subject gratefully.

Nick, feeling he'd won a victory by her agreement to stay two weeks, was perfectly willing to let her change the subject.

Ten minutes later he turned off the road, pulling onto a blacktop driveway. For a moment, a huge clapboard house was illuminated in the headlights before he cut the engine, plunging them into total darkness.

Gina blinked. "If that's a cottage, what do you call a house?" And more important, how was one person supposed to clean something that big? she wondered.

"My great-grandfather built it as a summer house, and summer houses are always called cottages by the locals no matter how big they are," Nick explained.

She glanced around in the stygian blackness and shivered at the house's isolation.

"This looks like a stage in a science fiction movie," she muttered. "I wouldn't be a bit surprised to find an alien lurking in the corners."

"I would," he said dryly. "Any being smart enough to build interstellar spaceships would be far too smart to have anything to do with mankind."

"Good point," she admitted.

"Watch your step." Nick used the irregular footing of the path as an excuse to give in to his growing compulsion to touch her.

Gina swallowed uneasily as his fingers closed around

the bare skin of her upper arm. His touch made her feel both excited and safe at the same time, which made no sense. The excitement she could understand. Nick Balfour was a very exciting man. Especially given her limited experience. It was the feeling of security his touch brought that confused her. She knew full well that security didn't come from outside. It came from within. Not only that, but she didn't know this man. Not really. So why did she find his touch so reassuring?

Confused, she watched as Nick unlocked his front door. Maybe her whole reaction to him was nothing more than a temporary aberration? Maybe tomorrow morning she'd wake up, take one look at him in the cold, hard light of day and wonder what on earth she had ever seen in him. Other than the fact that he was ruggedly handsome, tall and well built. Very well built.

"Welcome to my humble abode." Nick's voice broke into her thoughts. He flipped a switch just inside the door, and light flooded the entrance hall, momentarily blinding her.

Blinking to clear her vision, she followed Nick through the archway to the right into what appeared to be the living room, and looked around curiously.

About twenty by thirty, it was painted a depressing, mud color and was filled with comfortable-looking, stuffed furniture that had clearly seen better days. Early Salvation Army, she labeled the room's decor, wondering how well paid Nick was when he was working. Or was it simply that this was what he was used to and he hadn't noticed the general air of shabbiness? It was possible. She remembered a few of her girlfriends complaining about their husbands' refusal to part with old, worn-out chairs because they were comfortable.

Between the pair of French doors on the opposite wall,

there was a table with a large television on it. Beside it was a VCR and an elaborate stereo system. On the floor underneath were stacks of videos, DVDs and CDs.

Surreptitiously, Gina studied Nick as he tossed the truck's keys on the dusty surface of the end table beside the door. Somehow, the house didn't quite mesh with her initial impression of him. But she wasn't quite sure why, and she was much too tired to try to figure it out at the moment.

"You can see why I need a housekeeper," Nick offered into the growing silence.

Yes, she could certainly see that, she thought ruefully.

"Upstairs there are eight bedrooms and a bath. I sleep in one and use another as a study. There's also a bedroom and bath downstairs off the kitchen. You can have it."

Gina blinked. Eight bedrooms and one bathroom? That must have caused a few problems in the mornings.

"Come on. I'll show you where your room is," Nick said.

Gina followed him through the archway to the side of the living room and into a huge kitchen.

"The kitchen's kind of…" Nick waved his arm around the room.

Gina winced. It certainly was. The room reminded her of the before pictures of a renovated, inner-city house she'd seen featured in the Sunday papers a few weeks ago.

"My mother threatened to gut this room and completely remodel it, but my dad refused to hear of it," Nick confided. "He used to say that, if it was good enough for his father, it was good enough for him."

"Your mother has my heartfelt sympathy," Gina said.

"Oh, she took care of the problem," he said. "When

they retired and moved to Florida, she gave the house to me, and I don't mind. I mean, Dad was right in a way. My great-grandmother used to prepare meals here with no trouble.''

''Your great-grandmother also didn't have penicillin,'' she shot back. ''That doesn't mean she was better off.''

''Does that mean you don't like it?'' Nick glanced around, and Gina's heart constricted at his uncertain expression. Poor man, he probably couldn't afford to even replace the World War II–era appliances, let alone remodel the whole room. It was hardly kind for her to make him feel bad about it.

''It'll do just fine for the short time I'll be here.'' I hope, she added mentally with a jaundiced look at the ancient gas stove.

''Where is my room?'' she asked. ''And may I borrow a pair of your pajamas?''

Nick felt his entire body clench at the thought of her intense femininity actually inside his clothes.

Down, Balfour. You give her even a clue as to what you're thinking, and she'll be out of here so fast you won't even see her go.

''Sorry, I don't use pajamas,'' he said. ''How about a T-shirt instead?''

Gina swallowed at the captivating thought of his body sprawled out on his bed wearing nothing at all.

''That's fine.'' Her voice sounded odd to her, and she rushed on, hoping he hadn't noticed. ''I think I'll go to bed now. I know it isn't all that late, but I've been driving since six this morning, and traveling always makes me tired.''

Gina winced as her breathless babble echoed in her ears.

To her relief Nick didn't seem to notice.

"I'll get you a T-shirt then. Your room is through there." He pointed to a hallway behind her. "And sheets for your bed are in the linen closet in the bathroom."

"Just leave the shirt on the kitchen table," Gina told him, and then beat a hasty retreat to her room. She desperately needed some time alone to regain her normal equilibrium. Exploring life's possibilities was a lot more nerve-racking than she would have thought.

Chapter Three

Gina rolled over and opened her sleep-fogged eyes to find herself staring at a mustard-yellow wall. She frowned slightly, trying to figure out why a motel chain would paint anything such an unappetizing shade.

Not a motel! She jackknifed up as she suddenly remembered that she was in Nick Balfour's house. Her breath escaped in a relieved whoosh as she studied the chair she'd wedged under the knob of her bedroom door. It hadn't moved an inch. She'd been almost certain she could trust Nick, since both the waitress and the sheriff had vouched for him, but it was still nice to know she'd been right. Particularly since her judgment of people and their motives certainly hadn't been all that great to date.

She picked up her watch from the bedside table and checked the time.

Eight-fifteen. Was she late or early? She frowned slightly. She had no idea what kind of schedule a housekeeper normally kept. Nor, she suspected, did Nick Balfour.

Nick Balfour. Gina closed her eyes to better concentrate on the mental picture forming in her mind. She imagined that he was staring down at her with a look of intense interest on his rugged face. His dark hair was slightly rumpled as if he'd been running his fingers through it, and his pale gray eyes burned with desire.

A flush washed over her body, shortening her breathing. The man should come with a consumer-warning label attached.

Not that she needed one, she assured herself. She didn't want the complications an intimate relationship would bring. She didn't have the time or the energy to deal with them. She had to be back in Illinois by January seventeenth. But until then she was free. Free to try to learn some of the things that her girlfriends seemed to have been born knowing.

And it was certainly past time for her to indulge in a little experimentation, she thought, as she retrieved her underwear from the radiator where she'd draped them last night after washing them out in the bathroom sink.

She could count on one hand the number of dates she'd had in the past four years. And her social life before that hadn't exactly been anything to write home about.

A kick of excitement twisted through her at the thought of doing a little experimenting with Nick. Always provided he looked as good in the clear light of day as he had last night. She tried to dampen her expectations.

Gina winced as she slipped into her plain cotton underwear. They were cold, clammy and still slightly damp. First item on the agenda was to buy herself some clothes, she thought, mentally marking her to-do list.

She finished dressing, quietly removed the chair from

in front of her door, eased it open and paused to listen. It was funereally quiet. Either Nick was normally a silent man or he was still asleep.

Not still asleep, she realized as she peered into the kitchen and saw him standing in front of the sink, staring out the window at the overgrown garden.

Compulsively, her eyes traced over the width of his shoulders, which this morning were covered by a pale blue denim shirt with the cuffs turned back. Her mouth dried as she studied the dark hair that covered his left arm, and her fingers tingled as she tried to imagine what his firmly muscled flesh would feel like beneath her exploring hands. Savoring the freedom to study him unawares, she let her gaze slowly slip over his flat hips and then down the long length of his khaki-covered legs. He was so gratifyingly tall. She could actually wear heels and not tower above him. She had a brief vision of herself in a slinky black cocktail dress and thin, strappy heels, being held in his arms as they slowly danced around a moonlit terrace.

And like every other tall man she'd ever known, he probably preferred women built like Tinkerbell, she thought ruefully.

"Good morning." She tossed the greeting at his back.

He spun around as if startled to discover another person in the house with him.

Gina barely suppressed a wince. Instead of eagerly waiting for her to wake up, he seemed to have forgotten her existence. And to think she'd barricaded her door against him. The thought rankled. Just once she'd like a man to look at her and be consumed with good old-fashioned lust. Just once. Instead, she got a man who seemed to be desperately trying to remember where he knew her from.

Nick stared at her, caught off guard by the depth of desire that swept through him at the sight of her hovering in the doorway. His eyes lingered on the soft length of her chestnut hair, which barely brushed her shoulders. It looked shiny and silky. His palms itched to stroke it. To thread his fingers through it. To take a handful of it and to bury his face in it, and drink in the very faint floral fragrance he remembered from last night.

And as for what he wanted to do to the rest of her... His eyes slipped lower, lingering on the thrust of her breasts. She was eminently touchable. And even better, she was tall enough that he wouldn't get a crick in his neck trying to kiss her. She would fit perfectly in his arms.

But not in his life, he reminded himself. He already had a very demanding mistress, medicine. He simply didn't have the time to dance attendance on a woman.

Mentally he winced as he remembered the tantrums he'd had to endure, the one and only time he'd been stupid enough to try to balance the demands of his profession and a relationship. The vitriolic arguments and recriminations every time he'd been late had turned his life into a minefield. It was not an experience he cared to repeat. It had been a bitterly learned lesson, but at least he'd learned it.

On the other hand, the situation he found himself in now wasn't normal, he rationalized. He had more time to fill than he knew what to do with. And Gina was someone who could help him fill it. Even if he couldn't risk getting emotionally involved with her, they could still be friends for the short time she'd be here.

His mind immediately supplied him with an image of her lying in his bed gazing up at him with languorous eyes. He hurriedly sliced off the thought.

"Good morning," he finally said. "There's coffee if you'd like some." He nodded toward the half-full pot on the gray Formica counter.

"Thank you." She gratefully headed toward the caffeine only to be distracted by a whiff of his cologne. It was spicy and seemed to perfectly match the bright fall day outside. His scent made her think of crisp, chilled air and warm kisses in front of a blazing fire.

Determinedly she shoved the tantalizing thought to the back of her mind and, picking up the pot of coffee, poured herself a cup.

So much for her having exaggerated her attraction to him, she thought ruefully. If anything, her response to Nick was even stronger this morning than it had been last night. The question was, What was she going to do about it? Or, more accurately, What could she do about it? It was all well and good for her to decide to explore an emotional relationship with him, but to actually do it, Nick would have to cooperate. That was the sticking point.

Don't worry about what might happen, she told herself. First, deal with what was. And heading the list of things that needed to be dealt with was her stolen car.

"Did the sheriff call?" she asked.

"No. Not that I expected him to. I doubt he gets out of bed much before ten o'clock on a weekend."

"The joys of small-town living," she said dryly.

"Human nature is the same no matter what the size of a town," he said. "It's just that the behavior is more visible in a small town because there are fewer things to get in the way of seeing it."

"I'd sure like to know where you have to go to get away from crime if small towns aren't safe," she said.

"Heaven?"

Gina sighed dispiritedly. "Probably. This whole thing has sure taken the bloom off my big adventure."

"That's right. You said you were running away from home. Why?" He slipped the question in.

"Why what?"

"Why were you running away from home?"

"Because I'd rather be somewhere else. Didn't you ever want to chuck it all and take off into the wild blue yonder?"

Nick frowned slightly as he considered her words. "Not really," he finally said. "I've often had the impulse to chuck a few people off into the wild blue yonder, but I've had no desire to go there myself."

Odd, Gina thought. She had thought he would have found living in this run-down house in the back of beyond stultifying. Day after day of doing nothing. Going nowhere. Personally, she'd be a basket case after a few months of it. So why wasn't he longing for a change?

"You like living here?" she asked curiously.

"I'm being driven out of my mind!" His vehemence shocked her. "And I can't go back to work until my arm is healed. And even then, I'll have to have physical therapy to regain the dexterity in my fingers. It'll be at least another eight weeks before I can work again. Maybe longer."

Always provided he did regain his manual dexterity. Nick swallowed on the cold metallic taste of fear clogging his throat. If there had been nerve damage…

He shoved his long fingers through his thick black hair, and Gina found her eyes following the movement. Wondering about the texture of his hair. Fantasizing about what it would feel like if she were to touch it.

"What exactly did you break?" She stared at the imposing cast that covered his right arm from wrist to elbow.

"My radius," he said shortly, having no intention of telling her that it wasn't just a simple break. That the bone had been fractured into eight pieces by a bullet. Telling her that would lead to other questions. Questions he didn't want to answer.

"I see," Gina said slowly, wondering what he'd been doing when he'd broken his arm. Skateboarding? Skiing? Riding a motorcycle? But despite her intense curiosity, his almost palatable withdrawal discouraged any more questions. And she most emphatically didn't want him to start thinking of her as nosy. Regretfully she changed the subject.

"About this job you were kind enough to offer me."

"Kind, hell!" he broke in. "It was self-serving of me. If I have to spend one more day staring at the walls and eating my own cooking, I'll run screaming into the woods. I figured you'd be willing to put up with the house because you needed a place to stay."

"There's always a motel," she couldn't resist pointing out, having no desire for Nick to take her for granted.

"Not around here there isn't. They're all filled to capacity until after the fall foliage season is over."

Gina's lips twitched at his smug expression. "Like I said, I prefer a trade to a job. How about if I keep the part of the house you actually live in reasonably clean and cook two meals a day? You can choose which two. In exchange, you provide room and board and take me out to do some shopping this morning. Or loan me your truck, so I can go myself if you don't want to go."

"The trade is fine, but as for letting you drive Octavius..."

"It's only a truck," she said at his horrified expression.

Nick shuddered at what he clearly saw as rank heresy. "Octavius is a classic. You need to understand his quirks. I'll take you. It's not like I've got anything else to do. And I want lunch and dinner. I'll get my own breakfast."

"Do you have a schedule?" Gina asked.

"Schedule?" he repeated blankly.

"Yes, do you take have to take medicine or…" She gestured ineffectively.

"There wasn't a secondary infection, and the break can heal without any outside help."

Gina ran the tip of her tongue over her lower lip as she contemplated what else his body could do.

Snap out of it, girl. She pulled her overactive imagination up short.

"Did the doctor tell you to exercise?" she asked, latching on to a safe subject.

"For a broken arm?"

"Exercise is what you need," Gina said.

"There's a law about practicing medicine without a license," he said grumpily. He hated wasting time exercising when he could be reading case notes or studying the latest surgical techniques.

"Ha, grouchiness is a sign that you're bored."

"I am not grouchy!"

Gina suppressed the sudden urge to smooth away his scowl with her lips.

"Condemned out of your own mouth," Gina said, feeling exhilarated at her ability to hold her own in their conversation. Relating to men wasn't all that hard after all. At least, it wasn't as long as she remembered to treat him like a friend and not like someone whose bones she wanted to jump.

"And for your information, Nick Balfour, exercise is the cure-all in today's modern world. Everything is better if you exercise. Don't you read?"

"Do you believe everything you read?" he asked, unable to maintain his ill humor against her happy expression. Especially not when he knew she was right. His grumpiness was caused by boredom. He found the forced inactivity frustrating in the extreme. He wanted to be back at the hospital operating.

But even if he couldn't work, he was well enough to do things with Gina. He swallowed as he felt his body begin to respond to the sudden images that flooded his mind of just what he'd like to do with Gina.

He walked over to the counter and poured himself another cup of coffee to hide his physical reaction from her. If he wasn't careful, he would frighten her off, and then he'd be stuck here by himself again.

Gina was by far the most interesting thing or person he'd run across since he'd arrived here three weeks ago. She absolutely couldn't be allowed to escape.

"Surely you aren't suggesting that someone would actually print a lie!" Her bright blue eyes danced with impish lights, and her mouth curved into a smile that made him happy. He wanted to pull her into his arms and cover her mouth with his. To absorb her infectious good humor. To warm himself with her joy. Just being around her made the day seem brighter.

"You wouldn't happen to be one of those exercise fanatics, would you?" he asked suspiciously.

"Do as I do and not as I say," she replied primly. "I haven't been sick."

"I wouldn't call breaking an arm being sick. Besides,

haven't you ever heard that you're supposed to pamper injured people?'' Nick said.

''Sorry. I belong to the 'keep a stiff upper lip and get on with it' school of thought,'' Gina said, even as her mind was busily considering just how she would like to pamper him. She'd stick him back in bed and then she'd...

She was about to tell herself not to waste her time daydreaming when she realized there was no reason why she shouldn't. If she wanted to fantasize about Nick Balfour, then she could do it. In fact, if she wanted to do more than fantasize about the man, she could. Provided she kept the fact that she had to be in Illinois in four months in mind. The problem was that around Nick she found it hard to keep focused on future goals. His personality made the present too vivid, too overwhelmingly important.

''You should take up a program of gentle exercise,'' she persisted.

''I hate exercise.''

''People who exercise are healthier than those who don't,'' she countered.

''Platitudes the woman gives me.'' Nick addressed the ceiling.

''I tried facts, but you wouldn't listen to them.''

''How about if you exercise with me?'' Nick eyed her cagily, thinking one of two things would happen. Either she'd drop the subject or she'd go with him. Either way he won.

''What kind of exercise?'' she asked cautiously.

''How should I know? You're the one on the fitness kick. You choose.''

Gina briefly weighed the discomfort of exercising

against the pleasure of doing it in Nick's company and decided a little sweat was worth it.

"Maybe walking?" she suggested. "Walking seems to be the exercise of choice."

"Not my choice," he grumbled, "but I guess I can put up with it."

"Do you take a nap in the afternoon?" she asked, mentally trying to figure out when would be the best time to fit a walk into their day."

"A nap!" He looked down his nose at her. "How old do I look?"

"About two years... Oh, you said how old you looked, not how old you were acting, didn't you?" Gina gave him a bewitching smile that completely dissolved his annoyance.

Gina watched the twinkle in his eyes with a feeling of relief. Good, the gorgeous Nick Balfour could laugh at himself.

"I kind of walked into that one, didn't I?" he said ruefully.

"Chin first. What about breakfast?"

"I said I didn't want you to fix it for me."

"I'm not going to. I'm going to fix it for myself."

"Actually I haven't been bothering with breakfast," he said. "So I don't think there is anything to eat."

Gina bit back her opinion of that piece of dietary stupidity. She'd already won her point about exercise. She'd save the spiel about the necessity of eating a good breakfast till tomorrow.

"Well, if we haven't got anything to eat for breakfast, why don't we go pick me up a couple of changes of clothes and stop by the grocery store on the way back," she said.

"Sure."

Gina watched as he drained his cup of coffee, rinsed it out and set it on the counter. He certainly was a neat man. Had he learned it from a woman? But not a wife. Gina remembered the waitress at the bar had said he wasn't married. But he could have a girlfriend. The sudden thought sent a chill shivering through her. Simply because she wasn't here with him now didn't mean anything. She could have a job. Or kids who couldn't leave their school.

Uncertainly Gina nibbled on her lower lip. So how could she find out if Nick was committed to anyone without coming right out and asking? She might be free to live her life as she wanted to, but she didn't want to poach on anyone's relationship. Maybe… An idea occurred to her.

"How many should I plan on when I'm fixing lunch and dinner this weekend?" she tried to make the question sound businesslike.

"Just me and you. I'm supposed to be taking a complete break so I didn't tell anyone where to reach me. Uninvited guests can be very exhausting."

"So can invited ones," Gina said, trying to keep the excitement she felt out of her voice. Nick wasn't committed to anyone. He was fair game. And she had him dead in her sights.

Suddenly life seemed full of intriguing possibilities.

Chapter Four

Nick waited until Gina had dealt with the stiff seat belt before he started the truck.

"What do you need to buy?" he asked.

Gina considered the fact that all she owned at the moment were the clothes she was wearing and then said, "Everything. Is there a department store within reasonable distance? And a grocery store?" She remembered the state of his pantry. Mother Hubbard would have been right at home in it.

"You should be able to get everything you need in Vinton," he said.

"Sounds good," she said. "Let's get the shopping out of the way this morning so we can go for a walk in the afternoon."

Nick shot her a quick glance, his eyes lingering on the determined tilt of her chin. "You aren't going to turn out to be a nag, are you?"

"Hopefully I won't have to. Hopefully you'll take up exercising because it's the smart thing to do," she told him. For some reason it was important to her to think that he'd be better for having known her. And taking up exercising would make him healthier.

Nick gave her a quick grin that accelerated her heartbeat.

She took a deep breath to try to combat the sensation, but all that accomplished was to drag the tangy fragrance of his cologne deep into her lungs, further muddling her thoughts.

"Nice try, but if that theory worked, the cigarette manufacturers wouldn't have a market. Nor would the junk-food makers, nor…"

"I get the idea," she said dryly. "What I was trying to say was that I hoped you were bright enough to do what was necessary without my having to nag you."

"When did you start having these fantasies about me?" he asked.

The minute I laid eyes on you, Gina thought. And her fantasies had nothing to do with his mind. They all involved various parts of his gorgeous body. Like imagining his firm lips against hers. Unconsciously she shifted in her seat as she could almost feel the pressure of his mouth. Could almost feel the strength of his arms molding her to his broad chest.

"I still think you should let me buy your clothes." Nick's deep voice broke into her unsettling thoughts.

"And I still think you shouldn't," Gina refused. Not only wasn't she sure he could afford it, but she was determined to keep their relationship that of equals. If she started accepting money from him they wouldn't be.

"How about if we plan on going for a walk after I make my phone calls?" she said, refusing to allow him to change the subject.

"What phone calls are those?" Nick asked, intensely

curious about who she wanted to call. She hadn't mentioned a man but that didn't mean she didn't have one she wanted to stay in touch with. A woman as attractive as Gina must surely have someone lurking in the background somewhere. The thought rasped over his nerves, making him feel edgy.

"To the sheriff, the insurance company and the traveler's check people." She sighed dispiritedly. She hated paperwork, and she had the nasty feeling that before she got this whole thing straightened out she was going to have to fill out scores of forms. "Although, maybe I'll get lucky. Maybe when I call the sheriff, he'll say that the state police have found my car."

"I doubt it," Nick said truthfully.

"Pollyanna you aren't."

"If by that, you mean I face facts, then yes, I'm no Pollyanna. Or no, I'm no Pollyanna as the case may be."

"Whatever," Gina dismissed the whole thing. "Tell me what you like to eat."

"Food," Nick said succinctly.

"Can you narrow it down a little? Even a food group would help."

"I loathe chicken of any kind, barely tolerate fish and like desserts. Does that help?"

"Yes, it tells me you're a dietitian's nightmare."

"And I can't stand tofu," he added.

"If you don't like chicken and fish, it makes sense you wouldn't like tofu."

"Why is that?" Nick asked blankly.

"Because chicken, fish and tofu are good for you, and you clearly don't like things that are good for you."

"Now that is a calumny," he said. "I simply know what I like and I haven't yet been bludgeoned into silence by the health food fanatics."

Gina frowned slightly as she considered his use of the word *calumny*. That was not a run-of-the-mill word. In fact, she couldn't ever remember anyone using it in speech before. And she had worked in a business office full of people sporting their masters' in business and other assorted degrees. So what did Nick's choice of words mean? Probably nothing, she finally decided. For all she knew he could be a voracious reader. Just because she hadn't noticed any books lying around the living room didn't mean there weren't any. With eight bedrooms upstairs he could have the equivalent of a public library up there.

All his vocabulary proved was that there was more to Nick Balfour than met the eye. Gina stole a quick glance at him, her eyes lingering on the way the taut material of his slacks hugged his muscular thighs with an almost greedy intensity. And what met the eye was impressive enough. A woman could feast on his body for a long time without ever considering his mind.

Mentally she cringed at the sexist thought, but the plain, unvarnished truth was that Nick Balfour's body fascinated her, and if that made her a shallow person, then so be it.

"This should have everything you need," Nick's voice dragged her out of her thoughts, and she blinked, surprised to find herself in a parking lot in front of a large redbrick building.

Nick cut the engine, climbed out of the truck and went around to open the door for her.

Gina gave him a smile, feeling self-conscious at his old-fashioned manners. She wasn't used to men who opened doors for her, and she wasn't sure how to react. So she contented herself with a simple thank-you.

Gina walked across the parking lot beside Nick, enjoying the crunch of the leaves beneath her feet.

"It's a gorgeous day," she said happily.

"That it is," Nick agreed.

"Do you have any laws that forbid burning leaves?" she asked, mentally picturing a bonfire with marshmallows.

"No, what I have is common sense." He opened the door to the department store for her.

"A small fire isn't going to pollute the atmosphere," she argued.

"Not as long as it stays small, and I'm not worried about the atmosphere, per se. What I'm worried about is that it might get out of hand and I could lose the whole house before the fire department could do anything."

"I hadn't considered that," Gina admitted. "I guess it comes from living in a big city like Chicago."

"You've always lived there?" asked Nick, slipping the question in.

"Actually, I've always lived in the southern suburbs of Chicago." Gina stopped at the store's floor map beside the elevator and studied it. Sportswear was listed as being to her left.

"What are you getting first?" Nick asked as he trailed along behind her.

"A couple of outfits. It won't take me long."

It didn't. Gina quickly picked up two pairs of jeans, added three shirts, two sweaters and a package of white socks.

"Aren't you going to try anything on?" Nick asked her as she headed toward a cash register.

"No, I've bought these brands before. I know they'll fit."

Gina handed her pile over to the sales clerk along with her credit card.

"What next? A dress?" Nick asked, suddenly filled with a desire to see her in something silky, which would caress the long length of her legs. In red, he decided. A thin, red silk dress with a deeply cut bodice that would show off her breasts.

"No. All I want is some everyday clothes until I either get my car back or the insurance company pays me for what was stolen."

Nick frowned, reluctant to give up his visual image. She'd look great in a dress, but if he offered to buy it for her, she'd refuse. For some reason she was determined not to take any money from him. Hell, she'd even refused a salary for cleaning his house.

Nick's eyes narrowed when he caught one of the furtive little glances she was giving him. Now what? he wondered as he watched an enchanting pale pink color wash up under her skin. She was clearly embarrassed, but he couldn't see why she should be.

"Um, do you have anything you need to pick up?" she asked.

"No," he said.

"Oh. Well, would you mind amusing yourself for a few minutes?"

"I find you amusing enough."

Gina blinked, not sure how to take that. It sure didn't sound like the response of a man who had the least bit of romantic interest in her. At least, she *thought* that amusement and romantic interest were mutually incompatible ideas. But since her personal experience with sex was nil, she couldn't be absolutely sure. Even so, she refused to let it bother her. She had time to try to get Nick to see her as a sexy woman. And she intended to try very hard. She'd never met a man who appealed to her as much as Nick did.

"Where to next?" Nick asked.

"I'm going to the underwear department. Alone," Gina added. "I don't need an audience."

Nick swallowed as his body instinctively clenched at the tantalizing thought of watching her try on lingerie.

"How about if I meet you at the front door in twenty minutes." Nick forced the words out.

"Done." Gina hurried away.

She finished her lingerie shopping in just under fifteen minutes and hurried down to the first floor to find Nick.

She paused by the perfume counter when she caught sight of him standing by the front entrance. She allowed her gaze to trace over his body, relishing the sight of each luscious inch of him. He looked gorgeous, and he was all hers. Sort of. Reality dampened her initial burst of pleasure. But even though her time with him was limited…

Her train of thought was derailed when a slender blonde with legs that went on forever sauntered up to Nick. Gina was too far away to hear what the woman said to him, but she was certainly close enough to read the open invitation on the blonde's face. Outraged, Gina watched as the woman moved closer to Nick while she made a great show of checking out the directory.

Gina tried to swallow her rising sense of fury telling herself not to be ridiculous. So what if other women hit on Nick. He owed her nothing. He was free to respond or not as he pleased. The truth of her words made no difference to her emotions. She didn't want other women coming on to him. She sagged in relief when Nick moved slightly away from the blonde.

Hoping that none of her agitation was still visible in

her face, Gina hurried to meet him before he changed his mind about the blonde.

"All finished?" he asked.

"Yes," Gina said with a guarded look at the blonde who was lingering in front of the directory. To her astonishment the woman was eyeing her with a distinct expression of envy. It was the first time in Gina's lifetime that anyone had ever envied her her escort.

"Want one?"

Gina looked down into the white paper sack Nick held out to her. It was filled with chocolate. At least a pound and it looked like...

She took one and looked closer before she blissfully ate it. It was Godiva chocolate. And Godiva chocolate wasn't cheap. So why was he buying expensive chocolates instead of a candy bar if he wanted a chocolate fix?

She didn't know, and she could hardly ask him. How he spent what money he did have was not her business. A sense of frustration filled her. So much connected with Nick was not her business.

"Thank you, this is good," Gina said.

"You're welcome. I got some for later, too."

"You got enough there for all week and probably next week, too."

"Chocolate is good for you," he insisted. "It produces the same endorphins as being in love does."

"Oh?" Gina muttered as she considered his words. Endorphins were something to do with strenuous sports, and they were supposed to make you feel good, weren't they? So how did endorphins fit in with being in love? And how did Nick know about them if he didn't exercise?

She had no clue, nor could she think of any way to ask him without making it sound as if she was surprised that he knew anything at all. One thing she was sure of, first chance she got, she intended to check out those eight bedrooms upstairs and find out if he had a stash of books to account for his odd store of facts.

"We'll stop at the grocery store next," Nick said as he put her purchases behind the truck's front seat.

Gina checked her watch. It was barely eleven-thirty. They were making excellent time. With luck they should be back home before one o'clock and have the rest of the day for other things. A shiver roughened her skin as an image of Nick's lean features filled her mind. His image was taut with desire, consumed with a need that only she could fill.

"You ought to put on one of those sweaters you bought," Nick said, noticing her involuntary movement. "You don't want to catch a chill."

Gina chuckled. "I can just see someone with a catcher's mitt trying to snare themselves a chill. And once you capture it, how do you take it? Do you breathe it in or swallow it or absorb it through your skin?"

Nick looked down into her laughing blue eyes and felt a flash of desire explode in him. He wanted to pull her into his arms and feel her slender length against him.

"Besides, I don't believe in chills," she said, the matter-of-factness of her voice providing a brake on his raging hormones. "I think they're just an old wives' tale. You know, like, 'Feed a fever and starve a cold.' Or telling a kid, 'If you get your feet wet, you'll catch cold.'"

"Is that what your mother told you?" Nick asked, fascinated by her impish expression.

"No," Gina said shortly as all her good humor drained away. Her mother had never worried about her health. She'd been far too busy playing the role of an invalid, who needed to have her every want catered, to spare a thought for anyone else.

Nick frowned, wondering what he'd said that had brought about such an abrupt change of mood. One minute she'd been teasing him and the next she'd looked as if he'd just told her that the IRS was going to audit her tax return. Could her reaction somehow be tied to her wandering around the countryside with everything she owned in her car? He had the distinct feeling that something was very wrong in her life, but he didn't know her well enough yet to push the issue. She would undoubtedly go on the defensive and clam up. He needed to give her time to learn to trust him, and then maybe he could find out what she was running from and help her.

Nick waited until Gina had removed the price tags from a blue cardigan, put it on and had fastened her seat belt before he started the car. Five minutes later they arrived at the grocery store.

"I buy groceries here, and get milk and bread as I need it from the convenience market at home," he told Gina as he parked the car near the entrance.

Home? Gina tasted the word and found it oddly seductive. What would it be like to have a home with someone you loved? Someone like Nick. She stole a quick look at Nick out of the corner of her eye as they walked into the grocery store. Her imagination wasn't equal to the task.

"Do you want anything in particular for dinner?" Gina asked as she pulled a cart out of the rack of them just inside the door.

"I don't like chicken," he said.

"I already know that," she muttered. "How about spices?"

"I like cinnamon and ginger and cloves and nutmeg."

He reached over and placed his hands on the cart beside hers.

Gina shivered as his fingers brushed against hers, and she hurriedly relinquished her hold on the handle.

"I'll push the cart, you fill it," he ordered.

Gina swallowed, willing the odd fluttering sensation in her stomach to settle.

"What do you normally fix yourself for dinner?" Gina tried again. Maybe the way to a man's heart really was through his stomach. Not that she wanted Nick's heart, she assured herself. She had plans that made that idea impossible. But even so, it would be nice to have his attention focused exclusively on her for a while.

Nick thought of his habit of grabbing dinner at the hospital before going home for the day. He couldn't remember what he usually ate because it all pretty much tasted the same. Bland, overcooked and totally uninteresting.

"I usually just grab something to eat in the cafeteria after work," he finally said.

Cafeteria? If his place of employment had a cafeteria, then it had to be pretty big. Was it a factory? He'd said he was a technician, but that could mean anything. Could he be a tool-and-die maker? Or maybe he ran a very technical piece of machinery? She didn't know, but she would, she vowed. She was going to know everything there was to know about the fascinating Nick Balfour before she left. She just didn't want to ask him any personal questions at the moment. Their present accord was too precious to endanger by bringing up a subject he'd already proved reluctant to discuss.

"Tell you what," Gina finally said. "How about if I just try out dishes, and you can tell me afterward if you never want to see them again?"

''Just don't try out any chicken.''

''It's a deal,'' Gina said and began searching her memory for dishes that might appeal to a man. She'd cooked her mother's dinner every evening after work because her mother had insisted that she was too frail to do it herself. But what her mother had liked had been light meals. Nothing that would appeal to a man well over six feet tall.

Absently she began to toss groceries into the cart, eager to get back to the house. Once she'd made her phone calls, they would have the rest of the afternoon to do other things.

A frisson of insecurity suddenly ambushed her. Maybe he didn't want to do anything with her and was too polite to come right out and say so?

Determinedly, she pushed the feeling away, refusing to allow it to take root. It might turn out that he didn't fancy her, but she wasn't going to automatically make that assumption. She was going to act as if she were worth knowing, and maybe he'd believe it. And maybe if she told herself often enough, she'd believe it, too.

Just as she'd learned to believe her mother's constant jibes about how awkward and gawky she was. For as far back as Gina could remember, her mother had lamented having a lanky beanpole for a daughter. But she wasn't too tall for Nick, she comforted herself. He was a good six inches taller than she was.

Gina allowed her unsettling thoughts to drift away as they approached the checkout counter.

They made it home shortly before one o'clock, and after a quick lunch of sandwiches and canned soup, Gina cleaned up the kitchen while Nick disappeared upstairs.

Gina watched him go. She had the odd feeling that he was escaping from her. She told herself not to be silly.

That developing paranoia was not part of her game plan. A little caution when dealing with a man was good. Second-guessing his every move for a hidden motive was just plain stupid.

Once the kitchen was spotless, she headed toward the living room. First she'd make her phone calls and then she'd do a little housework. Then when Nick came back downstairs, she'd suggest they take a walk together. And if he hadn't reappeared by the time she had finished, she would go get him. An almost euphoric feeling of anticipation surged through her.

Thirty seconds into her phone call to the insurance company, her feeling of euphoria was gone, evaporated by the heat of her anger. Her second call, this time to the bank that had issued her traveler's checks, increased her anger, and by the time she'd talked to the sheriff, she was fast approaching fury.

Nick paused in the doorway of the living room and frowned slightly as he caught sight of Gina. Her whole body was rigid as if only extreme effort on her part was keeping her from exploding into a million tiny pieces.

As he watched, she carefully hung up the phone. The very care with which she did so was in stark contrast to the expression of impotent rage on her face.

"A problem?" he asked cautiously.

"No, not *a* problem," she bit out. "Problems in the multiple."

"What happened?" Nick asked.

"What didn't happen!"

"Tell me about it, and maybe I can help."

Tell him about it? Gina looked at him in surprise. She hadn't shared her problems with anyone since... She frowned slightly trying to remember. Not since her father had been diagnosed with cancer. He'd had far too many problems for her to burden him with hers. And her mother had never shown the least interest in her problems. Not even when Gina had been a small child. As far as her mother was concerned, she was the only one who had a right to have problems. The people around her certainly didn't.

"I make a very good listener," Nick's deep voice flowed soothingly over her agitated nerves.

That wasn't the only thing she'd bet he'd be good at, Gina thought as she eyed him longingly. But as for confiding a problem...

Why not tell him? she suddenly decided. Her problems at the moment weren't personal. Maybe he could point out something that she'd missed.

"Okay," she said. "You asked for it. Number one. My insurance company said that they will not issue a replacement check for my car until either thirty days after the filing of the police report or until they find it wrecked."

"Did they say why?"

"They gave me some song and dance about how lots of cars turn up after a few days because someone takes it to go joy riding and then dumps it in an out-of-the-way place."

"I could see holding off a few days for that reason," Nick said, "but thirty seems a bit excessive."

"That's what I told her."

"And she said?" Nick persisted, when Gina just stood there glaring at the wall.

"That thirty days was company policy and that some other insurance companies make you wait forty-five, and that she wasn't responsible for company policy."

"Which probably made you feel guilty for getting angry at her in addition to your anger over their policy,'' Nick guessed.

Gina gave him a curt nod. "Not only that but the rider on my policy that pays for a rental car in case of theft is only good for three days. Then when I called the sheriff to ask for a copy of the police report to send them, he said it wasn't ready yet because his wife was at her mother's!"

Nick frowned slightly as he considered her words. "I assume that Thelma is the one who does his typing?"

"I don't know," Gina bit out. "I was too angry to ask. I was afraid once I got started, I'd say a whole lot more than I intended, and he'd stall even longer just to get even."

"What about getting your traveler's checks replaced without the numbers?" Nick asked.

"They'll do it, but it takes a manager's signature, and there's no manager in the office on the weekends."

"I told you before, I'm perfectly willing to pay you a salary," Nick said, trying to ease her frustration.

"And I told you, I don't want a salary. I just want to trade some cleaning for room and board," Gina insisted. She was determined to keep the playing field between them level, which she couldn't do if he was her employer. As his employee she couldn't treat him as a sexy, desirable man, and she wanted to. And she intended to, just as soon as she figured out how to do it…subtly. She didn't have either the experience or the nerve to come right out and tell him she fancied him like mad. Besides, if she tried the blunt approach and he turned her down, she'd not only be mortified, but staying with him would be impossible.

"But the final aggravation was that I couldn't reach the lawyer handling my father's estate. I did get his answering service to call his home, but his wife said he'd just stepped out. You'd think at least one of my phone calls would have had a positive result!"

Nick studied her pale, tense features for a long moment and then said, "You need to relax. Stress is bad for you."

"Tell that to the people dumping it on me."

"You can't control them. You can only control your reaction to them," he said.

Gina closed her eyes a moment, then opened them and said, "I just tried explaining that to myself, but myself isn't buying it. I still feel angry enough to scream."

"I learned a technique for relaxing when things get too intense. Want me to show you?"

"Sure, I'm willing to try anything at this point."

Nick moved closer to her and said, "First breathe in through your nose and slowly exhale through your mouth.

"No, not like that," he said as she took a shallow breath. "You need to breathe deeply. To completely fill your lungs. Let me show you."

He slipped his hand beneath her shirt and placed his hand against the bottom of her rib cage.

"Try again," he ordered. "And this time take in enough air to make my hand move."

Gina tried to concentrate on what he was saying, but it was impossible. Every brain cell she possessed was focused on the feel of his hard fingers burning against the soft flesh of her diaphragm. Her heart was racing at the erotic sensation, and it was all she could do not to lean into him to increase the light pressure he was exerting.

Blindly she stared at the small, white button on his denim shirt as she struggled to match his level of so-

phistication. Clearly touching her wasn't even register-
ing with him. He sounded exactly the same as he always
did while she didn't dare try to talk for fear she'd sound
as shaken as she felt.

"You're still not taking a deep enough breath," Nick
said.

"Sorry." Gina forced out the word. Desperately, she
dragged in air and then almost moaned with reaction as
his fingers flexed. If it felt this good just to have him
touch her, what would it feel like if he were to make
love to her?

"That's better. You just need to practice the technique," he said, removing his hand.

"Practice," Gina muttered distractedly as he turned
away. She'd practice anything if he touched her while
she was doing it.

"You work on breathing for a few minutes, and I'll
make us some coffee," Nick said.

He left the room, hoping it wasn't obvious to her that
he was escaping. Once in the kitchen, he pressed his
fingers against the bridge of his nose and tried to figure
out just what had happened in there.

He'd been sympathetic to her obvious frustration.
He'd wanted to ease it. To help her recapture the happy,
relaxed mood she'd been in all morning. So he'd decided
to teach her the technique he used to relieve the stress
he felt during long, tricky operations. When she hadn't
quite had the breathing technique right, he'd placed his
hand on her diaphragm to show her how she should be
doing it.

And from that point, everything had gone haywire.
The minute he'd touched her, he'd been inundated with
the most compelling urge to hold her and kiss her. He'd
wanted to jettison deep breathing and relieve her stress

in the most basic way possible—with sex. It had been
all that he could do not to pull her up against him and
kiss her until she didn't have a thought in her head but
him. The only thing that had stopped him was the fact
that he was afraid she'd cut and run if he did. He'd
offered her a safe haven while she was sorting out the
mess created by her car's theft. Sex certainly hadn't been
part of the deal. She might even think that he expected
sexual favors in exchange for a place to stay.

Grimly Nick filled the coffeepot, still trying to make
sense of his reaction to touching Gina. It was unprece-
dented. He touched women all the time in his job. And
the only thing he ever thought of when he did it was
what he could do to solve their problems. He never reacted to them sexually. So what was different about
Gina?

She wasn't his patient, for one, he decided. But then,
lots of women weren't his patients, and he didn't react
to them the way he did to Gina. What made her different?

Maybe it was simply hormones, he told himself. He
was a normal male, and Gina was an attractive woman.
A very attractive woman. And he was living in close
quarters with her. It wasn't that unusual that he should
want her. There was nothing wrong with that. At least,
there wasn't as long as he kept it firmly in mind that his
attraction couldn't go anywhere.

In a month or so he'd be back in Boston to start his
physical therapy, and after that he'd be inundated with
work again.

If his bone healed properly, and if the therapy worked
on his torn muscles, and if there hadn't been any nerve
damage. Fear sent a cold chill through him. He had to
be okay because if he wasn't...

A black cloud of despair engulfed him at the thought of never operating again.

"Nick, phone for you."

Gina's voice pierced his depression, and he latched on to it like a lifeline. Switching on the coffee machine, he hurried back to the living room and Gina.

Chapter Five

"I need to make a phone call, and then how about if we take our walk?" Gina said when Nick had finished his call.

An image of her locked in his arms in his bed upstairs immediately formed in Nick's mind. No doubt about it, his idea of exercise was a whole lot more fun than hers.

His body tensed as he watched her slender hand reach for her cup of coffee. She had the most gorgeous hands. He wanted to place a kiss on each and every fingertip and then press her hand flat against his bare chest, but he couldn't. Even though they were both adults and free to indulge their desires, he knew making love to her would be a bad idea. A very bad one.

Just kissing her would be all right, he consoled himself. Provided she was willing, but so far he'd seen no sign that he'd even registered with her as an available male. Which wasn't surprising since she'd been in a state of emotional turmoil ever since he'd rescued her in the bar. He needed to give her a chance to settle into some kind of normal routine, and then he could subtly test the waters and see if she might be agreeable to getting to know him a little more intimately.

He swallowed uneasily as he watched her fingers curl around the blue mug and raise it to her soft pink lips. A stab of pure lust shafted through him as he imagined her lips pressed against his body instead of an unappreciative piece of pottery.

Down, Balfour, he told himself. Keep it light.

"Who do you have to call?" he asked in the hope that words would deflect his mind's fascination with her body.

"I want to try one more time to reach the lawyer who's handling my father's estate. I want to give him this address so he can express me a check. That way I won't have to worry while the insurance company drags its feet. Which I suppose makes the insurance company one up on the sheriff. He doesn't appear to have even realized that he has feet to drag!"

Nick chuckled at her aggrieved expression. "Bitterness will get you nowhere."

"I wonder where a good shove would get me," she muttered.

Nick used her words as an excuse to allow his gaze to sweep down the length of her body.

"Considering how slender you are and how portly our esteemed sheriff is, he probably wouldn't even notice."

Slender? Gina considered the word he'd used and found it infinitely more satisfying than the *lanky* her mother always used to describe her figure. *Slender* made her sound as if she could be desirable.

Gina peered at Nick over the rim of her coffee cup. His features were impassive, not giving her a clue to his thoughts. He was not a man who allowed his feelings to show. That was probably just as well, she thought wryly, since she'd wasted his morning shopping and was about to drag him on a walk.

But the walk, at least, was for his good. And hers, she admitted with a total lack of self-deception. It would give her a chance to work on her skills at relating to an attractive man.

Anticipation surged through her, and she hastily gulped down her coffee so she could get her phone call out of the way.

"It shouldn't take more than a couple minutes for me to make my phone call," Gina said, trying to sound casual.

She most emphatically didn't want Nick to realize just how much she enjoyed being in his company. He might begin to worry that she would turn into a pest, and regret his offer to let her stay. Or, even worse, he might pity her. Her skin crawled at the thought. Indifference she could handle. She'd certainly had enough practice dealing with masculine disinterest. But pity she couldn't take. It would destroy her already fragile ego.

Picking up the phone, Gina carefully dialed Mr. Mowbry's number. To her relief, his answering service connected her with his residence the minute she identified herself. It was the only thing about the call that went smoothly. Instead of agreeing to express her money immediately, he told her that he couldn't do so because her mother was contesting the will.

Gina bit hard on her lower lip to keep from saying what she really thought. Her mother might be monstrously selfish and incredibly self-centered, but she was her mother and Gina had no desire to expose her family problems to an outsider. Even one who was supposedly representing her legal interests.

"Can she contest it?" Gina finally asked.

"She can do anything she wants. I think what you really mean to ask is can she win?" Mr. Mowbry said precisely.

Gina ignored what she saw as nit-picking and said, "So can she?"

"I doubt it," he said. "It isn't as if your father didn't more than adequately provide for her. It's just a shame that you didn't complete your degree while he was still alive." His voice held disapproval. "I'm sure it would have meant a great deal to him to have seen you graduate."

Gina gritted her teeth against the impulse to tell him that having her home to take him to his doctors' appointments and to his chemotherapy and to read to him when his vision became affected by his treatments had undoubtedly meant more to him. All things that her mother had so charmingly claimed she simply couldn't do because her father's illness had devastated her.

From the disapproval she could hear in Mr. Mowbry's voice Gina had no doubt that her mother had already twisted the facts of her father's devastating illness in order to paint herself as a long-suffering wife who had been forced to deal with a willful daughter.

A sense of impotent anger filled her. Why couldn't she have had the kind of mother everyone else seemed to have? The kind who actually liked you for yourself instead of seeing you as some kind of inanimate prop whose only function was to serve as a servant. Failing that, why couldn't other people see her mother for what she was? Why did they always buy into her "helpless little woman bravely coping with a selfish daughter who wouldn't listen to reason" ploy?

"Not that it's my place to criticize your actions," Mr. Mowbry offered into the growing silence.

"No, it isn't, is it," Gina snapped as her anger briefly surfaced. She paused a moment to get it under control, and then said, "It is your place to fulfill the terms of my father's will and that involves giving me my bequest. As soon as possible."

"You must understand that dealing with a will that is contested takes time." His voice cooled perceptibly, and she could almost hear him thinking that her mother had understated how unreasonable Gina could be. But for once she didn't care. She was right, she knew she was right, and she intended to act on that knowledge. Her mother and Mr. Mowbry were just going to have to deal with it as best they could. Her days of meekly falling into line to placate her mother were gone.

Maybe there really was something to that old saying that knowledge could set you free. Once that doctor had told her that her mother was perfectly healthy, Gina had felt as if the weight of the world had been lifted from her shoulders. Never again would she have to feel guilty about her mother.

"Not only do I need some of that money now, but I'll need enough to pay for tuition in January," Gina warned him.

"I'll try to get a court date soon, but…"

"You might tell the judge what I need the money for, and that my mother is trying to stop me from returning to school."

"But that isn't true!" Mr. Mowbry sounded shocked by her charge.

"Then what would you call what she is doing?" Gina bit out.

"Your mother is worried that you'll get in with the wrong crowd again and—"

"Again!" Gina yelped. "Mr. Mowbry, you are in danger of being taken for a fool."

Instead of getting mad, Mr. Mowbry sighed. "Your mother said you were very bitter and that you blamed her for not realizing your father had cancer earlier, but if you would just think, you'd realize that there was no way she could be blamed."

Gina drew a shaky breath, knowing she was fighting a losing battle. Never in a million years would she ever be a match for her mother's sly, manipulative behavior. There was no reason to even try.

"Mr. Mowbry, I'll give you till the end of September and if you haven't gotten a court date by then, I intend to find another lawyer. One whose loyalty is to me, not my mother."

"I hardly think…"

"That much, my dear sir, is discouragingly clear! I'll check back with you in a few days."

Gina gently replaced the phone, when her every impulse was to slam it down. And then to throw a screaming fit. She ground her teeth together in frustration.

"Let me guess." Nick's soothing voice slipped across her furious thoughts, knocking the edge off her anger. "The lawyer was behaving like a lawyer?"

"Like a stupid lawyer," she muttered. For an instant she was tempted to tell him about her mother. About her half-truths and outright lies, but the impulse died stillborn. He probably wouldn't believe her. No more than her mother's doctor had believed her.

"Is there anything I can do to help?" Nick asked, wanting to do something to erase her tormented expression.

"No." Gina gave him a determined smile. "Nothing short of an act of God could make the courts hurry up." She gave him part of the truth. "And that being so, I refuse to dwell on it."

Nick grinned at her. "It's a great theory. Are you going to be able to put it into practice?"

"Yes." Gina nodded emphatically, determined to have a positive attitude no matter what. Her mother's self-serving games might have warped her past, but she refused to allow them to poison her future.

"I'll exercise my frustrations off."

"How far are we going to walk?" Nick asked as he followed her out the back door.

"Not far." Gina took a deep breath of the crisp, fall air. The pungent scent helped to soothe her frazzled nerves. "I want to get back and do some cleaning and start on dinner."

"How far is not far?" Nick persisted.

Gina frowned thoughtfully. "I read an article once that said one should be able to walk three miles in forty minutes. That seems reasonable."

Nick kept his doubts to himself. "How far is three miles?"

"Fifteen thousand odd feet?"

"Which of us is going to count?" he said.

Gina chuckled. "Not me. I'll be too busy breathing."

"We need one of those pedometer things that measures how far you walk."

"What we need is perseverance," Gina shot back. "How far we walk isn't as important as the fact that we do it. Let's say we walk out twenty minutes and then turn back."

"Okay," Nick agreed. "What about stretching exercises?"

"Stretching?" Gina stared blankly at him, not seeing a tall man in a denim shirt and well-cut chinos. Instead, her ready imagination saw the body beneath the clothes. The naked body. Enthralled, her mind watched as his body reached above his head making the muscles in his flat abdomen contract. His broad chest was covered with the same dark hair that decorated his uninjured arm. His...

"One stretches to avoid a muscle pull." Nick seemed oblivious to her distracted expression.

"I don't have any muscles to pull." Gina regretfully allowed her imaginings to drift away.

"Everyone has muscles," he argued.

"Ah, but there're muscles and there're muscles. Do you know any stretching exercises?" she finally asked.

"A couple. We could also warm up by starting slowly and then building up speed."

"That's it," Gina agreed. "Start out slow and work up to it."

They could start out with a kiss and work their way down to... Her gaze slid over his flat stomach, and a quick surge of heat engulfed her. Don't go there. She hastily yanked her gaze away from the temptation of his body.

"I'll keep track of the time." Nick fiddled with his watch. "There. It'll alert us when it's time to turn back."

Gina glanced down at his thin gold watch with its brown leather band, nestled in the dark hair on his wrist. Instead of being digital, it had hands. It looked faintly old-fashioned and very expensive, she decided, as she noted how thin it was.

"Somehow that doesn't seem like the kind of watch I'd expect you to have." She muttered her thoughts aloud as she lengthened her stride to match his.

"Why not?" Nick asked.

"You said you were a technician. I would think you liked technology. So I would have expected you to have a digital watch complete with a dozen functions."

Nick frowned. He didn't want to tell her the truth. That a second hand made taking a person's pulse easier. Which left what? Another half-truth.

"I like this one. It suits my needs."

"What kind of technician are you?" Gina asked, risking a personal question.

"I fix machines that are malfunctioning," he paraphrased one of his medical professors who had claimed that the human body was the most fantastic machine ever engineered.

"Do you like your job?"

"I love it." There was no mistaking the sincerity in Nick's voice. Or the faint air of desperation as he added, "I would never be happy doing anything else."

"Why would you change?" Gina instinctively responded to his tone of voice even though she didn't understand it. Had he had a girlfriend who had been embarrassed that he repaired machines for a living and tried to talk him into doing something a little more white-collar? If so, the woman had been stupid.

"You're lucky to have found something you really like to do. I feel that way about children who have reading problems," she confided.

"You want to teach kids who can't read?"

"Kids who can't read are few and far between. More common are kids who have some degree of dyslexia. Reading for them is difficult. Those are the ones I want to work with."

Nick glanced down at her face, his attention caught by the enthusiasm glowing in her blue eyes. She'd make an excellent teacher, he realized. Patient and kind, with an underlying enthusiasm that would shine through everything she did. An enthusiasm that would communicate itself to her students.

"You'd make a great teacher," he voiced his thoughts aloud.

"Thanks," Gina said, rather surprised by his response. Virtually everyone she'd told about her desire to work with challenged children had rambled on about how frustrating she'd find it. About how the lack of mental stimulation in a job like that would bore her out of her mind within months. Nick was the first one who had simply accepted what she'd said. Not only accepted it, but had told her that he thought she would do well at it.

A bright glow of pleasure engulfed her.

"What grades do you plan on working with?" he asked.

"Early primary. The quicker you get to a kid with a reading problem, the easier it is to fix it. By the time they're in middle school, their attitudes about reading are set in stone and it takes blasting powder to change their minds."

Gina was so caught up in what she was saying, she forget to watch where she was going and tripped over a partially buried rock. Hastily reaching out for something to steady herself on, her fingers closed around Nick's denim-covered arm. Convulsively her fingers clenched, digging into his hard muscles. He might not exercise, but he felt as if he was in great shape, she thought distractedly.

Nick hurriedly used his broken arm to awkwardly steady her against his body.

"Are you all right?" he asked.

Gina stared at the top button on his shirt, her eyes

lingering on the crisp dark hair on his chest she could see above it. Her fingers tingled as she imagined what it would feel like to thread them through that hair. To rub the palm of her hand across it. To...

"Gina?"

"Yes, I'm fine," she hurriedly dragged her gaze away from temptation. "I just tripped and lost my balance."

And almost lost my common sense, she chided herself as she clenched her hands into fists to try to quell the longing to touch him.

"Maybe we should walk on the road next time?" Nick suggested.

Gina stared into his eyes, her attention caught by the tiny flickers of light gleaming in them. Almost as if a candle flame were illuminating them from behind, the fanciful thought occurred to her.

"But the road has cars, and they can be a much bigger hazard than natural obstacles in the woods." Nick answered his own question when she remained silent.

Gina's gaze slipped from his eyes to land on his mouth. She watched, fascinated by the way his lips moved as they formed words that echoed meaninglessly in her ears. What would it feel like if he were to kiss her? Would his mouth feel as good as it looked? Would...

Her breath was suspended in her lungs as his lips moved closer to her. The warmth of his breath washed over her face, and a sense of intense longing filled her. She felt the heat of his lips brush across hers like a brand, and she jumped in reaction.

"Better?" he asked, and the word echoed oddly in Gina's ears.

Better? she thought in confusion. Frustrated would be a far more accurate description of how she'd felt. She didn't want an insubstantial kiss. She wanted him to kiss her properly. To take her in his arms and mold her body to his.

But clearly he didn't want the same thing or he would have done it. The unpalatable thought depressed her, but she refused to allow herself to be discouraged. They were supposed to be exercising, not indulging in love-making. And if his casual kiss had seemed more like the kind of salute exchanged between friends than lovers, it was a start, she assured herself. Who knew where it might end. She had time. She would be here for weeks before everything was straightened out with the insurance company. Anticipation added a spring to her step.

"Maybe we ought to drive into town and try walking on sidewalks?" Nick suggested.

"Driving somewhere to exercise seems silly." Gina tried to sound her normal self. She most emphatically didn't want him to realize just how strongly she had reacted to his kiss. He might think she was some pathetically repressed spinster, and she wasn't. She just hadn't had any opportunity to experiment. She stole a glance up at his face, and excitement shivered through her. Yet.

"The list of anomalies in modern-day living would reach from here to Vinton," he said dryly. "It used to be people got enough exercise just going about their daily life."

"I've been to a few museums where they had people hauling water out of wells, chopping wood with an ax and cooking over an open fire." Gina shuddered at the memory. "I have no desire to live in the so-called good old days."

Nick chuckled. "Where's your sense of adventure?"

"It was locked up by my common sense," she said

tartly. "How far do these woods go back?" she asked curiously.

"Miles, although only a couple hundred acres of it are mine. The rest is state forest." Nick glanced at his watch when it emitted a discreet beep. "Time to turn back."

Gina obediently turned around. "I think we should pick up the pace," she said.

"The footing isn't very good," Nick said. "You've already tripped once."

"But the scenery makes up for any small deficiencies. I'll bet it'll still be gorgeous in a few weeks when the leaves are all off."

"You can't walk in the woods then," he said.

Gina waited for an explanation and when none was forthcoming asked, "Why not?"

"Hunting season starts. Being in the woods then is asking to be shot."

"Shot!" Gina stared at him in shock. "What on earth kind of hunting do you have in this state?"

"It isn't the hunting that's the problem. Most hunters are responsible, but a few are fools who'll fire at anything that moves and ask what it was after they've shot it." Although it wasn't just in the woods that fools with guns caused grief, Nick thought grimly as he stared down at his cast.

"So much for the perfect environment," she muttered.

"Nothing is perfect," Nick said flatly, and Gina had the odd feeling he was talking about something else entirely.

She stole a quick glance at his shuttered face and shivered. It was as if he had suddenly put out Do Not Trespass signs on himself. And she lacked both the nerve and the social skills necessary to break through his sudden reserve.

Stifling a sigh, she plodded along beside him.

"Would you like me to start my cleaning upstairs?" she asked once they were back at the cottage.

"No, I've got some things I need to do in my study, so concentrate on the downstairs."

And don't bother me, she mentally added.

"Okay." She forced a cheerful note into her voice. "I'll clean the upstairs bath and your bedroom tomorrow morning."

"That's fine. Just don't do anything in my study. I know where everything is, and if you clean I might never find some of my stuff again."

"Have you ever heard of a filing cabinet?"

"I have a system, and it works just fine. I'm going to make some fresh coffee, you want some?"

"I'll have mine later," Gina said.

Smiling at him, she walked out of the kitchen and left him to his coffee making. Much as she wanted to be around him, she didn't want him to think she had ulterior motives. Such as lusting after him. Even if she did. Although... She remembered his sudden withdrawal during their walk. Could it have been caused by his realizing just how strongly she had reacted to his casual kiss? Could he have been trying to tell her not to get ideas?

Embarrassment shivered through her. She didn't know if that had been his reason, she told herself. His reaction could have had nothing to do with her. But just to be on the safe side, she'd have to be very careful not to let him see how strongly he affected her.

Chapter Six

"There you are."

Gina pulled her hands out of the dishwater and turned at the sound of Nick's voice in the doorway. For a long, self-indulgent moment she simply feasted her eyes on him. He was wearing a pale blue, cable-knit sweater that contrasted attractively with his dark hair. He really was a spectacular-looking man, she thought dreamily. The wonder was that he wasn't already spoken for. He must be an expert at discouraging women before they got too possessive.

A flush scorched her cheeks at the humiliating thought of being told to back off. He didn't have to worry about warning her off, she assured herself. She might have designs on his body, but they were definitely short-term designs. Come January she had to be in Illinois.

For the first time the thought of going back to school wasn't accompanied by a surge of excitement, and she found the fact disquieting.

"Have you been breathing cleaning fluids?" Nick studied her abstracted expression. "You look spaced."

Gina mentally stifled a sigh at his description. Just once she'd like a man to look at her and see someone irresistibly attractive. She might as well wish to win the lottery while she was about it, she thought ruefully as she dried her hands.

"The only cleaning stuff I've been using is soap to wash the dishes since you don't have a dishwasher."

"We have a septic system this far out of town."

Gina waited for him to elaborate and when he didn't asked, "What does that have to do with it?"

"I'm not sure, but that was always what my father told my mother when she said she wanted a dishwasher."

Gina giggled. "And if that excuse was good enough for dear old Dad, it's good enough for you."

"Yes, he… Sorry, I forgot why I was looking for you. You have a phone call."

It was odd, he thought, but when he was around Gina, all he could think about was her. Everything else went out of his head. He'd never had that response to a woman before, and that fact worried him. Although it shouldn't, he assured himself. There wasn't any danger Gina would to try to take advantage of his response by maneuvering him into a more permanent arrangement. She'd been very clear that she had to be back in Illinois by January.

"A phone call? Did they say who it is?" Gina asked as she hurried into the living room. Maybe the insurance company had decided not to make her wait the full thirty days?

"I didn't get a name." Nick followed her. "But it's a woman if that helps. She had a faint, breathy voice."

Gina froze with her hand almost on the phone as a feeling of dread iced her skin. Faint and breathy? Her mother always sounded like that. As if she didn't have quite enough energy to take a deep breath.

Gina tried to banish her sudden surge of fear. Her mother didn't know where she was. Her mother might be persistent, but she wasn't psychic. It was probably that woman from the traveler's check office she talked to last Saturday. She'd promised to get back to her on Monday when the manager was due in, and it was Monday.

Taking a deep breath, Gina picked up the phone and said, "Hello?"

"Gina, darling, who is that man who answered the phone?"

Gina felt the blood drain out of her face and a curious ringing sound echo in her ears. Blindly she stared at the dark brown wall opposite her and sucked in air.

You're an adult, she told herself. A self-supporting adult. Your mother has no hold on you. She swallowed a rising feeling of nausea, wondering how her mind could be so sure of the fact when her emotions weren't.

Nick frowned as he watched the color leech out of Gina's face, leaving the freckles scattered across her nose standing out in stark relief. Who was on the phone? he wondered. Could it be the traveler's check people telling her they wouldn't replace the checks without the serial numbers? But he wouldn't have thought that that news would have upset her quite so much. And she was upset. He noted the whiteness of her knuckles gripping the phone. She looked tense enough to break.

"Problems?" he asked.

Gina jumped as if she'd completely forgotten he was still in the room.

Covering the phone, she said, "No, it's not a problem."

Nick ignored his first impulse, which was to take her in his arms and tell her that he'd protect her. Her whole stance was one of dismissal, and he had to respect it. Trust couldn't be forced.

"If you want me, I'll be in the kitchen," he said, and left to give her the privacy she clearly desired.

Gina waited until she heard the kitchen door close, then said, "What do you want, Mother?"

"I want an answer," Helen demanded. "Who is that man who answered the phone and what are you doing there with him?"

Not what I wish I could do with him. I wish I could jump his bones. The irrelevant thought helped Gina to regain some of her normal equilibrium.

"Where did you get my phone number?" Gina countered with a question of her own.

"The lawyer. I explained that I needed to get in touch with you because my heart condition is worsening, so he gave it to me."

"I would definitely agree that your condition is getting worse if you called me here." Gina struggled to keep her voice even. Bitter experience had shown her that losing her temper only played into her mother's hands. "Tell me, have you considered seeing a psychiatrist to find out why you have such a need to control the people you profess to love?"

"I never thought you could be so unkind as to leave me." Her mother gave a watery sniff, and Gina could almost see her lower lip trembling. It was a technique she had used for years to get the response she wanted from either Gina or her father.

"I don't think you want to go there," Gina said.

"Moreover, I see no point to this conversation. I don't want to talk to you."

"I'm your mother, and I need you."

"It isn't a healthy need. Not for you and especially not for me. I'll be in touch later," Gina said, hoping that by Christmas she could face talking to her mother without giving in to her anger over the years she'd wasted dancing attendance on her.

"You didn't tell me who that man was!" Her mother's voice sharpened. "He sounds much too sophisticated for someone like you. I mean, I love you, darling, but even I have to admit that you have no sex appeal and…"

Gina carefully hung up and then stared blindly into space while she struggled to get her sense of anger and inadequacy under control. Her mother was sick, she told herself. She didn't mean what she said. Nor was it necessarily true. Granted, she didn't have the kind of sex appeal that made men stop dead in the street and stare. Nor did she have the pretty, blond delicateness that appealed to men's protective instincts like her mother did, but that didn't mean that she didn't have any appeal. All she needed to do was learn how to make the best of what she did have. And she would. Now that she was no longer spending every free moment catering to her mother, she would have time to explore her own femininity.

Gina gave a decisive nod of her head. And she was making a start. With Nick. He certainly didn't act as if he found her a complete turnoff. She shivered as she remembered that kiss in the woods on Saturday. Although since then, he hadn't touched her or even made a suggestive remark. Could that one kiss have been enough to convince him that he didn't want any more from her? She frowned at the deflating thought.

"Bad news?"

Gina spun around at the sound of Nick's voice in the doorway.

"Um, no. Not really. Just a minor glitch."

"Anything I can do to help?" Nick offered, relieved to see that some of her natural color was seeping back into her cheeks.

Not unless he knew a psychiatrist who made house calls in Illinois, she thought ruefully. And could figure out a way to make her mother admit that she had a problem that needed to be addressed.

"No, thanks," she said.

Wanting to change the subject, Gina glanced around the living room, searching for something to do now that the housework was finished. She couldn't see anything.

"What kind of hobbies do you have?" she asked in the hopes she could share one with him.

"I don't have time for hobbies. Normally I work a lot of overtime."

"Well, this is a good time to explore some interests," she said with determined cheerfulness. "What would you like to do?"

Pick her up, carry her off to the nearest bed and then make love to her all night long, Nick thought, trying to imagine how she'd look if he did that. Her eyes would be slumberous and her cheeks would have a flush and her soft mouth would be full and swollen and her breasts...

He hastily chopped off his thoughts as his body began to react. What was wrong with him, he wondered uneasily. He was becoming obsessed with her body. He needed to concentrate on her mind more. It was safer.

"There must be something you like to do?" Gina tried, refusing to be put off by his silence. Unless he came right out and told her to drop it, she intended to find something they could do together. She had no intention of passing up this heaven-sent opportunity to hone her male-relating skills.

"It's your idea. You pick something," he said.

"Okay, I will." Gina found the morning newspaper and opened it.

"If you're looking for a movie theater, there aren't any in town. We'd have to go to Vinton." He watched her, his eyes lingering on her slight frown as she read. He wanted to rub it away and then put a completely different expression on her face.

"Going to a movie isn't what I had in mind. I'm looking for the... Ah, here we go. The upcoming events calendar."

"We have an upcoming events calendar? In Wellingsford?" he asked in disbelief.

"Sure." Gina smoothed the paper out and studied the column. "From the sound of it, the people in this town lead a pretty hectic social life. The curling society is having a meeting tonight. Although I have no idea what curling is."

"It has something to do with ice and brooms," Nick said absently. "I saw it once in the Olympics. It didn't make a lot of sense to me."

"So how much sense does a bunch of grown men committing mayhem on a football field make in order to move a leather ball from point A to point B?" she asked dryly.

"That's different!" Nick said.

"Only because you happen to like football. To those of us who don't, one sport is the same as another."

"Philistine," Nick grumbled. "I'll take you to a football game, and then you can see the difference for yourself."

Gina suppressed the surge of excitement she felt at his invitation, if that was really what it was and not one of those male throwaway lines like "I'll give you a call."

"Anyway," he continued, "curling is out. I haven't been on skates since I was a kid. I'd probably wind up breaking the other arm."

Gina glanced at his cast. She'd forgotten all about it. She bent over the paper again.

"There are two possibilities, a lecture tonight at seven-thirty at the library on how to improve your child's IQ, and a ballroom dancing lesson tomorrow night at the town hall," she said, hoping the excitement she felt at the thought of being in his arms wasn't apparent in her voice.

"Kids are smart enough already," Nick grumbled.

"It sounds interesting, though," she said. "I wonder if the lecturer will have any ideas I can use for my students."

"Can't hurt to find out." Nick responded to the curiosity in her face. He checked his watch. "We'll need to leave now if you want to be there on time."

Gina jumped to her feet. "Have you got anything I can take notes on?"

"I'll get something from upstairs. Why don't you check to make sure the back door is locked while I do that?"

"Sure." Gina headed out to the kitchen and carefully tested the dead-bolt lock. It gave her a curiously contented feeling to perform such a mundane task. As if they really were a couple sharing the household duties before heading out for a good time. If going to a lecture could be classified as a good time.

Gina grinned. Going anywhere with Nick Balfour fell into that category. He was the most intriguing man she'd ever met. Not that she'd met all that many. But she had done a lot of observing from the sidelines over the years, and Nick Balfour was unique.

She made a quick detour into her room to grab one of her new sweaters and then rushed back to the living room. She slowed down when she saw him standing by the front door, not wanting him to realize how eager she was to go out with him. She wanted to appear cool and sophisticated.

She started through the door he was holding open for her only to come to a stop when she felt his hand on her shoulder.

"Stand still a minute," he said. "You've got…"

Gina tensed as his fingers brushed across the back of her neck. They felt hard and hot, and a shiver chased over her skin, raising goose bumps on her arms.

His hand suddenly slipped inside her collar, and her whole body clenched in reaction. She had to concentrate to remember to breathe in and out. In and out, she prodded her overloaded mind. The faint fragrance of his cologne drifted into her nostrils, further muddling her concentration.

"There," he exclaimed, handing her a small, white piece of cardboard. "You missed the price tag."

"Thank…" Gina winced at the breathless sound of her voice, firmed it and continued, "Thank you."

"No problem." He followed her out, then locked the door behind them.

It didn't take them long to reach the library, and Gina was impressed by the number of cars in the parking lot.

Apparently a lot of parents were eager to improve their children's intelligence.

Nick found a parking space, pulling his battered pickup in between two SUVs.

"Did the paper say who this lecturer is?" Nick asked.

"Just that she was a psychologist with a private practice in Vermont."

"I wonder what makes her an expert on IQs," Nick said.

"Interest? Knowledge isn't always measured by degrees."

"True, but neither is prejudice and bias measured by a lack of one," Nick said dryly.

"Sounds to me like you're the one with the prejudices. Don't you think parents should try to give their kids every advantage?"

"I think parents should let their kids be kids and stop trying to turn them into miniature Einsteins!"

Gina frowned, wondering at his vehemence. She found it hard to believe that he was jealous of anyone else's achievements. From everything he'd said he was very happy with his life, except for the forced inactivity caused by the broken arm. But maybe his parents were disappointed at his seeming lack of success? It was possible, she conceded. So many people equated success with a college degree, despite the fact that the average plumber not only made far more money than the average business major but the plumber performed a very useful function.

Since there was no possible way she could ask a question like "Are your parents disappointed in you?" she simply followed Nick into the library. They went up the back stairs and entered a medium-size meeting room filled with people.

Gina watched Nick casually greet several people as he made his way toward the back where there were empty seats.

Gina stopped when she caught sight of the sheriff sitting in the middle of the room.

"Hey." She grabbed Nick's arm. "There's the sheriff. I wonder if he has any news."

"No," Nick said.

"No, you don't wonder?" she asked.

"No, he doesn't have any news," Nick said.

"Pessimist," she said. "I'm going to ask him."

Gina waved to the sheriff, who obligingly heaved himself to his feet and came over.

"Heard anything yet, Ms. Tessereck?" Mygold asked her.

Gina frowned quellingly at Nick as he turned a laugh into a strangled cough.

"That's what I wanted to ask you, Sheriff."

"Oh, I thought the state police might have called you directly," he said. "Not that they take car theft all that seriously. Now, if you'd have been kidnapped with the car, then they would have jumped in with both feet."

"How remiss of me," she said tartly. "I didn't realize that the personal touch went so far in law enforcement."

"Well, it's the publicity, you see," Mygold told her earnestly. "A good kidnapping or a messy murder makes headlines, and headlines make careers. A car theft on the other hand is nothing."

"Allow me to assure you that, from the viewpoint of the victim, a car theft is something," Gina snapped.

Mygold gave her a vague smile and hurried back to his seat as a woman walked to the podium in the front of the room.

"I almost expected him to pat me on the head and

The Silhouette Reader Service™ — Here's how it works:

Accepting your 2 free books and gift places you under no obligation to buy anything. You may keep the books and gift and return the shipping statement marked "cancel." If you do not cancel, about a month later we'll send you 6 additional books and bill you just $22.84 per shipment in the U.S., or $26.18 per shipment in Canada, plus applicable taxes if any.* That's a savings of over 10% off the price of all 6 books! You may cancel at any time, but if you choose to continue, every month we'll send you 6 more books, which you may either purchase at the discount price or return to us and cancel your subscription.

*Terms and prices subject to change without notice. Sales tax applicable in N.Y. Canadian residents will be charged applicable provincial taxes and GST.

If offer card is missing write to: Silhouette Reader Service, 3010 Walden Ave., P.O. Box 1867, Buffalo NY 14240-1867

BUSINESS REPLY MAIL
FIRST-CLASS MAIL   PERMIT NO. 717-003   BUFFALO, NY

POSTAGE WILL BE PAID BY ADDRESSEE

SILHOUETTE READER SERVICE
3010 WALDEN AVE
PO BOX 1867
BUFFALO NY 14240-9952

NO POSTAGE
NECESSARY
IF MAILED
IN THE
UNITED STATES

start muttering about how I shouldn't worry my pretty little head about such things,'' Gina hissed in an angry undertone to Nick once they'd sat down.

Nick reached over, patted her head and murmured, "Now, now, my dear. You mustn't worry your pretty little head about such things."

Gina tensed at the feel of his hard fingers. Her scalp felt hot and tight, and her mouth dried. And all he'd done was pat her on the head. It seemed as if the longer she was around him the more sensitized she became to his touch.

Uncertainly she looked into Nick's eyes, seeing the laughter dancing in their gray depths. She had never felt less like laughing in her life.

Gina took a deep breath, trying to relax her tense muscles. Okay, so she'd gotten all hot and bothered by his casual touch. It wasn't a problem as long as she didn't let Nick realize just how much he affected her. Sharing Nick's home cried out for sophistication, and she was going to act sophisticated if it killed her. And she didn't have the slightest doubt that what she'd die of would be acute sexual frustration.

"You're skating on thin ice, my friend," she finally said.

"And I'm getting the distinct feeling that it's over very deep water, too," Nick said cryptically.

A voice from the front of the room called the audience to order, and Gina turned away from Nick in relief. Maybe if she concentrated hard enough on what the speaker had to say, she could successfully block out Nick's compulsive appeal long enough for her skittering nerves to calm down.

Opening her notebook, she waited for the speaker to

finish his long-winded introduction of Dr. Anderson, the lecturer.

Gina blinked when the lecturer rose from her chair and moved to the podium, taken aback by her appearance. Dr. Anderson was gorgeous! Drop-dead gorgeous. Gina stole a quick glance at Nick. He was watching the woman with an impassive expression. It was impossible to tell anything from his face. Maybe he didn't like tall, leggy blondes in clinging, black silk dresses, she thought hopefully. In short, clinging, black silk dresses that lovingly molded every lush curve the woman possessed.

Dr. Anderson didn't need to worry about her own IQ, Gina thought, all she had to do was stand there and nine out of ten males would fall all over themselves to give her whatever she wanted.

Gina winced, ashamed at the sexist thought. It wasn't Dr. Anderson's fault that nature had handed out beauty to her with such a lavish hand. The woman deserved to be judged by her ideas and not by her appearance.

With a massive effort, Gina forced herself to ignore how Dr. Anderson looked and to concentrate on what she had to say. A task that became harder about a third of the way through the lecture when Dr. Anderson discovered Nick's presence. From that point on, she seemed to address most of her comments to him personally.

Gina shifted restlessly. And the worst part of the whole thing was that coming here had been her bright idea. If it had been left to Nick, they would still be back at the cottage doing... Doing what?

The sudden image of Nick bent over her, his eyes gleaming with desire and his wide mouth curved in a sensual smile, slammed through her. She gulped, refusing to lose herself in the daydream no matter how delightful. She needed to pay attention.

But listening to Dr. Anderson's theories simply convinced Gina that she didn't agree with them. Her methods sounded so…cold-blooded.

Gina felt only relief at the enthusiastic round of applause that greeted the end of the lecture.

"Are there any questions from the audience?" Dr. Anderson smiled benevolently at them.

Yes, Gina thought, why did I let myself waste a perfectly good evening listening to you reduce kids to inanimate objects?

To Gina's surprise, Nick raised his hand.

"Yes." Dr. Anderson gave Nick the full benefit of her perfect white smile.

"On what factual evidence do you base your contention that IQ is basically set by the time the child is two?" Nick asked.

"In the course of my extensive practice I have found that trying to raise an IQ after two is rarely met with success," she said firmly.

"You would be aware, of course, that your theory runs counter to prevailing neurological studies," Nick said. "Particularly the best-known one in its field, Barton and Slycovski."

Barton and who? Gina blinked, wondering how Nick knew about them.

"I feel that particular study was fundamentally flawed," Dr. Anderson said. "As an expert in the field of child development, I can assure you that, if parents follow my methods, they will raise their child's IQ."

"Since IQ tests on very young subjects are notoriously unreliable, how do you measure results?" Nick asked.

"Don't worry. You'll be able to see the difference." Dr. Anderson gave him a seductive smile that made Gina furious. The woman was actually coming on to Nick. In front of everyone. Not that Nick seemed to have noticed, Gina conceded as she studied his impassive face.

"Are there any other questions?" Dr. Anderson turned to the rest of the audience.

A thin woman in the front asked a question about the flash-card technique that Dr. Anderson had recommended.

"Bingo," Gina muttered when she heard Dr. Anderson say that she had developed twelve different sets of flash cards and that they would be available for sale at the conclusion of the lecture.

"It's all about money," Gina whispered to Nick.

"It usually is," he agreed.

After the audience had finally run out of questions, Gina stood up, more than ready to leave.

"Did the lecture come up to your expectations?" Nick asked.

Gina wrinkled her nose in disgust. "I think it comes under the heading of 'You have to kiss a lot of toads before you find your prince.'"

Nick chuckled. "And are you looking for a prince, Gina?"

"No, princes are high-maintenance items, and I'm too busy to waste the time. Besides," she added thoughtfully, "I've never bought into the fantasy of some prince sweeping me up on his horse and riding off into the sunset."

"Why not?" Nick asked, curious as to how her mind worked.

"Well, think about it. First of all, it's demeaning. As if I couldn't make a life on my own, so some guy has to create one for me. Second, what rational woman would want to be married to a man so shallow that he picks out his wife solely on the basis of her looks?''

''I will admit that's not an aspect I'd ever considered before.''

''Hello there.''

Gina turned at the sound of the voice, and found herself staring into the most gorgeous violet eyes she'd ever seen. Contacts, Gina thought. But very effective contacts.

''I wanted to thank you for your insightful comments,'' Dr. Anderson leaned toward Nick, effectively shutting Gina out.

''I'm Beverly Anderson, and you are?'' She waited expectantly.

''Nick Balfour and this is Gina Tessereck.''

Dr. Anderson gave Gina a quick smile that was little more than a grimace, and turned back to Nick.

Gina watched, torn between fascination and fury. She might not like the woman hitting on Nick, but she sure wished she had some of her technique. Or her self-assurance. Of course, if she looked like Dr. Anderson, then maybe she would be that self-assured, too, Gina thought with a worried glance at Nick to see how he was reacting to the charm Dr. Anderson was slathering on him.

He wasn't. At least not outwardly. There wasn't a clue about his feelings to be read on his face. Because he didn't have any reaction to Dr. Anderson or because he didn't want to show what it was? Gina couldn't tell. All she was sure of was that he'd make a terrific poker player.

''If you have time later, I'd like to discuss the subject in depth with you.'' Dr. Anderson batted her lashes at Nick. ''I'm staying the night at the Windward Inn.''

"How lucky you are to have found a room during the peak foliage season," Gina threw in.

"I've found that if you're really determined, you can always get what you want." Dr. Anderson gave Gina a dismissive smile.

"Thank you, Dr. Anderson, but we need to be leaving," Nick said.

"Without having refreshments?" Dr. Anderson looked startled. As if being turned down by a local in the back of beyond wasn't a possibility she'd even considered.

"Gina," Nick drew her into the conversation, "are you determined to drink watery punch and boxed cookies?"

"No, I'd much rather leave," she said with absolute truth.

Nick took Gina's arm and, with a nod to the disbelieving Dr. Anderson, headed toward the door.

The warmth from his fingers ran through her like a tide, raising both her blood pressure and her heart rate. Her tongue darted out to run over her dry lips.

To her disappointment, Nick released her once they were safely out of the crowd in the meeting room.

Refusing to dwell on her increasing sensitivity to his slightest touch, Gina told herself she was just feeling unsettled because Dr. Anderson had made her feel insecure. And she *had* felt insecure. She doubted she'd ever be able to compete with the Dr. Andersons of the world. Not in looks and not in self-assurance. Gina mentally cringed as she remembered how she'd dithered over how to introduce herself to Nick in that bar. No doubt Dr. Anderson would have marched right up to him and told him how lucky he was that she was going to speak to him.

But on the other hand, she was the one now living with Nick, and Dr. Anderson was the one who had been brushed off. Politely, but that was what Nick had done, brushed her off. Gina found the thought very comforting.

Chapter Seven

Unobtrusively Gina studied Nick in the dim light of the truck's dashboard lights. He looked like a stranger. A mysterious stranger. A shiver skated over her skin, but it wasn't a shiver of fear, it was a shiver of anticipation. Anticipation at the prospect of plumbing the depths of Nick Balfour's personality. Of delving into the secrets of his body.

Her breathing shortened as her eyes dropped to his strongly muscled thighs. A wave of heat engulfed her, drying her mouth. What kind of lover would he be? she wondered. What would it feel like to be pressed against his naked body?

Gina swallowed as her breasts began to tingle, seeming to swell under the weight of the evocative thought.

"What did you think of the lecture?"

Nick's words echoed oddly in her ears as if they were coming from a distance. With a massive effort, she throttled her imagination and refocused on the reality of Nick's deep voice.

"Not much." To Gina's relief her voice came out sounding normal. She would feel humiliated if he were to realize just how obsessed she was becoming with him. She couldn't bear for him to think she was an emotionally immature woman who became completely flustered when faced with an attractive man. Because she wasn't, she assured herself. She might not have much experience, but inexperience and immaturity weren't the same thing at all.

"I was expecting something insightful and all I got was a hard sell for her flash cards," Gina said. "Can you imagine any mother being dumb enough to prop up a two-month-old baby and show it flash cards of all things?"

"Yes, unfortunately, I can," Nick said dryly. "What's worse, I think a lot of those mothers live right here in town. Did you notice the number of people buying her cards after the talk?"

No, I was too busy watching her hitting on you, Gina thought.

"I suppose they can't do any harm," she said slowly. "In fact, they might even do some good if the person were to hold the child while flipping those cards. Body contact is important to babies."

"Body contact is important to everyone." Nick's voice deepened perceptively.

Gina shifted restlessly in her seat as his dark voice rasped sensually over her nerves. Was his comment a double entendre? Was she supposed to respond to it if she wanted him to follow up on it? And if so, what kind of response was called for? A feeling of frustration gripped her. She didn't know. She would be wise to ignore the whole thing and opt for a safer subject. There was less possibility of embarrassing herself that way.

"You raised some very interesting points about brain development," Gina said, remembering something that had bothered her at the time. How had Nick known about that study? And known it well enough to quote it. She'd never heard of it, and she'd had a child development course. So where did a guy living in the back of beyond run across it?

"I was trying to inject a few facts into Dr. Anderson's assumptions, but they appear to have died from loneliness," he said wryly.

"Are you interested in brain development?" Gina probed.

"Not particularly."

"You seemed to know a lot about it for someone who isn't all that interested," Gina said, risking a more direct approach.

Nick frowned slightly, realizing too late that he should have kept his mouth shut. But listening to Dr. Anderson spout her theories as fact had infuriated him. He'd wanted to puncture the woman's smug, self-satisfied ego. And he should have known better. He met people of Anderson's ilk all the time in Boston, and nothing short of a cruise missile could penetrate their sense of superiority.

Now he'd made Gina suspicious. And he didn't want her suspicious. He wanted her to treat him as she had before the lecture. As a friend. He wanted her to talk to him as if she liked him, Nick Balfour, the man. Not Nick Balfour, the eminent surgeon, or Nick Balfour, the monstrous trust-fund baby. Being valued for himself was an intoxicating experience that he didn't want to give up until he had to. He wanted to bask in the feeling for just a while longer.

He knew things would change once he told her the

truth. Bitter experience had taught him that. He took his eyes off the road long enough to glance over at her, his gaze lingering for a split second on the way her full lower lip was caught between her teeth. As if she was worried about something. Such as his feeble explanation?

"I watched a television series on the brain one winter," he said, not telling her that the lecture series he was referring to had been during his third year of medical school.

"Oh." Gina imperceptibly relaxed at his explanation. "I imagine it was on NOVA," she said. "I've seen some fantastic series there, but I missed that one."

Nick felt both better and worse when she accepted his explanation. Better that she wouldn't probe anymore, and worse because he was finding it harder and harder to lie to her. Even when they were white lies. Gina was such an up-front person that he found himself wanting to match her honesty. But he didn't dare risk it. He had too much to lose.

When they reached the cottage, Nick turned into the driveway and cut the engine. With luck, by tomorrow Gina would have forgotten all about the lecture, he told himself as he climbed out of the truck. He certainly intended to.

As if she could read his mind, Gina said, "I don't think tonight was a success."

"Forget lectures," Nick agreed as he unlocked the front door and pushed it open for her to enter.

"I wouldn't go that far. I mean, just because this one was—"

"A front for a con artist?" Nick finished her sentence.

Gina giggled, and the enchanting sound slammed through Nick's body with the impact of a blow. He clenched his teeth against the impulse to crush her against him. He resisted the urge because he didn't think he could stop at just one kiss. He wanted to pick her up, carry her upstairs to his bed and make love to her all night long. And he couldn't. If he tried it, she'd probably cut and run. And he'd never see her again. The appalling thought gave him a sinking feeling.

You've been isolated out here in the woods too long, Balfour, he told himself. Once you get back to work in Boston, your fascination with Gina will fade. Strangely enough, the thought brought him no comfort.

Gina set her purse down on the table right inside the door and glanced at Nick. He was standing there with a grim expression on his face, which she suddenly found daunting. Feeling uncertain, she traced the impressive width of his shoulders. He would make a formidable opponent, she realized. She raised her gaze to the aggressive thrust of his jaw. Formidable and relentless.

But his expression had nothing to do with her, she rationalized, trying to calm her skittering nerves. Not only was she just passing through, but she had far too much sense to anger him. Nor did she think she had the ability to do it.

In order to really make someone furious, you had to either be important to them or be messing up something that was important to them. And she didn't know Nick well enough to know what he considered important. Nor was she stupid enough to believe that she was important to him. On any level. The thought depressed her even though she knew that it was for the best. She had to be back in Illinois in a few months, she reminded herself. She couldn't afford to do more than just skim over the surface of his emotions.

Gina glanced uncertainly at him, having the odd feel-

ing that the ice over his passions would be very thin and
if she fell in… She shuddered at the thought of the havoc
that would cause in her life.

"What's wrong?" Nick noticed her shudder. "Are
you cold?"

"No," she muttered.

Nick watched the emotions flittering across her face,
unable to read any except uneasiness. But about what?
he wondered in frustration. Surely he hadn't done anything to cause her withdrawal. Because she was doing
just that, withdrawing from him, and he found it infuriating. He didn't want her hiding her emotions from
him.

Slowly, so as not to startle her, he reached out, cupped
her chin in his hand and lightly ran his thumb over her
bottom lip. The sound of her hastily indrawn breath echoed loudly in the still air.

Nick felt the trembling of her soft flesh reverberating
through his body, intensifying his physical reaction to
her. It was all he could do not to kiss her until she didn't
have a thought in her head that didn't begin and end
with him and what he could make her feel.

"You must be tired," he said, pushing the tip of his
thumb every so slightly into her mouth. He clenched his
muscles against the almost overwhelming urge to allow
his tongue to follow where his finger was. To trace the
outline of her lips and slip inside. To taste her.

He stared down into her blue eyes, noticing how they
appeared to have gone all smoky. The pupils were huge
pools of black that appeared bottomless. A man could
drown in her gorgeous eyes.

"I think I'll go to bed," she whispered.

Nick heard the uncertainty in her voice and forced
himself to step back.

"Good night," he said, and resolutely turned and walked into the living room.

Gina watched him go as she struggled to get her pounding heart under control. Why had he touched her? And what had it meant? Or had it meant anything? Was she projecting her own desires onto his actions? Just because she craved physical contact with him didn't mean he shared her feelings. Maybe that seemingly casual touching had been exactly that. Casual. Maybe he'd meant nothing more than an adult did when they ruffled the hair of a child?

Gina stifled a sigh as she headed toward the kitchen and her own room. He couldn't be interested in her. From both the magazine articles she'd read and the comments her more knowledgeable friends had made, she knew that when a man was interested in a woman he made a move on her. He didn't casually touch her. He touched her purposefully. He tried to talk her into bed, and Nick hadn't.

Grimacing, she closed her bedroom door behind her. She refused to get discouraged. Simply because she hadn't yet managed to make Nick see her as a sexy woman didn't mean she might not eventually do it.

Catching sight of herself in the dresser mirror as she stripped off her sweater, she winced. The question was, How was she supposed to do that when she possessed none of the attributes that society said she needed to be thought of as sexy? Her body was too tall and too thin, her breasts were too small and her face too unremarkable.

She turned away from the discouraging image in the mirror. There had to be a way. Lots of skinny, nondescript women had boyfriends. They had to have found a way to project a desirable image, and if they could do it, so could she. Before she left here she was going to make Nick Balfour see her as a woman, she vowed.

"Gina?" Nick's voice came a second before the sound of his knuckles rapping on her bedroom door echoed in the room. "Are you in bed yet?"

Gina swung around. What did he want? Had he suddenly decided he wanted to kiss her good-night? The intriguing idea sent a ripple of awareness through her before common sense doused it.

Whatever he wanted, he certainly hadn't discovered an uncontrollable lust for her body in the past five minutes. No matter how much she might wish he had, she conceded.

Hurriedly yanking her sweater back on, she opened the door and said, "What's wrong?"

"Nothing, I just checked the messages on the answering machine, and there's one for you."

"The insurance company?" she asked hopefully.

"I don't know. It was some woman who said she really needed you to call her, that it was very important."

Gina tensed. "Did she leave a name?"

Nick studied her for a moment, wondering what had suddenly reduced her to frozen stillness. As if…as if she were afraid, he decided. But there had been nothing frightening about the message. Annoying perhaps. The woman had sounded cloyingly sweet, and he personally hated dealing with people like that, but that didn't mean Gina shared his aversion.

"No, she didn't," he finally said. "She simply said that she was very ill and asked you to call her as soon as possible."

"Thank you." Gina's voice was a thread of sound. "I'll call her in the morning."

"As you wish," Nick said and then left, wondering what was going on. The woman had said she was sick, and yet Gina wasn't reacting as if she was worried. No, that wasn't exactly true, he remembered her taut expression. Gina was worried all right, but he didn't think what was worrying her was the fact that the woman had said she was ill. The call itself was what seemed to have worried her. But Gina must have given the woman this number, otherwise she wouldn't have it. And if she didn't want the woman to call, then why had Gina made it possible for her to do so?

He didn't understand, and it bothered him. Nor did he like Gina shutting him out. He wanted her to tell him what was wrong. Was Gina in some kind of trouble? But what kind of trouble could she be in? A vision of her laughing features flashed through his mind. He refused to believe that she had done anything illegal. Which left what?

Nick opened the liquor cabinet and poured himself a whiskey. Picking up the squat tumbler, he walked over to the window and stared out into the blackness.

Could she be on the run from a bad relationship? His breath escaped from between his clenched teeth as an image of Gina in bed with another man flashed through his mind. Grimly, he banished the haunting image and tried to think rationally. His conclusion made sense when he thought about it. Not only had she been running away when he'd first met her, but it would also explain why she had all her possessions in her car. If she'd been living with some guy and they'd broken up, she would have been left without a home. And if she'd been the one who had decided to break it off, and he hadn't wanted her to go, that would explain why she hadn't

simply gotten another apartment in the same town. She'd
wanted to put distance between them.

But if that was what had happened, then where did
the woman who'd left the message tonight come into it?
Absently, he sipped his whiskey, trying to figure it out.
He couldn't. He didn't have enough facts.

Hell, he thought in frustration, he didn't have any
facts. All he had were impressions and guesses, and they
could be wrong. Gina's almost palatable withdrawal
when he'd given her the message could have had nothing
whatsoever to do with the message itself. She could have
had something else entirely on her mind. Although he
didn't know what it could be, when he'd been talking to
her not five minutes before, and she hadn't had anything
more weighty on her mind than the con artist they'd
listened to earlier.

Nick drained the rest of the whiskey and set the glass
down on the windowsill with a frustrated thump. He
wanted to take her in his arms and assure her that he
wouldn't let her past harm her. But he couldn't. If he let
her know that he cared, she might think he was emotionally involved with her.

And he wasn't, he assured himself. At least not much.
He simply liked her. All he wanted from her was companionship spiced with a few kisses. A surge of excitement shot through him at the memory of their earlier
kiss. Tomorrow he would try his luck again, he decided,
but this time he'd deepen it into a more intimate one.
His breathing shortened at the thought of really kissing
her. Of exploring the sweet essence of her mouth.

Tomorrow couldn't come soon enough as far as he
was concerned.

Gina was not of the same frame of mind. She tossed
and turned for hours until she'd finally managed to fall

into an uneasy doze punctuated by dreams in which her
mother arrived and dragged her home again.

As a consequence she woke up with a nagging head-
ache and the feeling that she was caught up in a recur-
ring nightmare.

Taking a couple of aspirins, she told herself to stop
being fanciful. She was an adult. A financially independent adult. No one could make her do anything she
didn't want to do. She had only to stand firm, and eventually her mother would give up and allow her to live
her own life.

Gina sighed as she made coffee. But right now she
was going to have to call and tell her mother to leave
her alone, and the necessity of it made her feel guilty.

You're programmed, she told herself. Programmed to
give in to your mother's every demand and to feel guilty
when you don't. And only you can break the chains. She
can only control your life if you let her.

Trying to hang on to the thought, Gina went looking
for Nick. He wasn't in the living room, and the house
was silent. Was he still asleep?

She glanced at the clock. It was a few minutes before
eight o'clock. She had no idea what time he'd finally
gone to bed last night. Only that it must have been after
she had.

She should return her mother's call before he came
back down, she decided. She certainly didn't want him
to overhear. Explaining about her mother was not a risk
she wanted to take. Not with Nick. Their accord was too
precious to risk damaging it.

Forcing herself to pick up the phone, Gina dialed her
mother. It was answered on the first ring as if her mother
had been camped beside the phone.

"Why didn't you call me last night? I distinctly told

you I was not feeling well. I could have been dead by this morning.''

"Sorry, but I'm not buying into that game anymore." Gina tried to keep all emotion out of her voice. "There is nothing physically wrong with you."

"I tell you—"

"No, for once in my life I'm telling you. Leave me alone."

"You are my daughter."

"Daughter and slave are not synonymous terms," Gina snapped, as anger began to nudge aside guilt.

"I'm ill," her mother repeated.

"Yes, and the kind of doctor you need is called a psychiatrist. I suggest you call one and make an appointment."

Gina carefully hung up the phone, shaking with a nauseating blend of anger and guilt.

"Good morning," Nick's deep voice came from behind her, and she swung around to see him standing in the doorway.

How long had he been there? she wondered, her gaze flying to his face. His mouth was curved into a smile, but his eyes... Gina felt a frisson of unease as she stared at his hard, watchful eyes. His expression had nothing to do with her, she told herself, trying hard to believe it.

"I was just starting on my daily round of phone calls," she tried to sound casual.

To her relief, he changed the subject, making no comment about the call she'd just made.

"Is there any coffee?"

"I just made a pot," she said.

"Good, I could use some caffeine." Turning, he headed into the kitchen.

Gina's tense muscles relaxed. He must not have heard her, or he would have said something.

Picking up the phone, she called the insurance company. Three phone calls and thirty frustrating minutes later, she put the phone down, when what she really wanted to do was slam it.

"Try that deep-breathing exercise I showed you," Nick said from behind her.

"I'm beyond deep breathing! I'm now into tantrums."

"Tell me about it."

"According to the insurance company, they can't even begin to process my claim until they have the police report, and they still haven't gotten it. The traveler's check people said that the manager is still held up in Akron. They hope he'll be in this afternoon but they aren't sure. And the lawyer who was supposed to send me some of my father's bequest hasn't been able to clear up a snag."

"Snag?" Nick asked.

"My bequest is being contested," she gritted out part of the truth. She didn't want to tell him that when she had called the lawyer to see if by some miracle her mother had changed her mind about contesting the will, she had had to listen to him lecture her about how unfeeling she was to abandon her poor, sick mother. It had been all she could do not to yell at the man to stop being so gullible. She'd wanted to tell him to call her mother's doctor and ask him just how ill her mother really was. The only thing that had stopped her was that she knew the doctor would never discuss her mother's health with the lawyer. Instead Gina had swallowed her fury and told him to tell her mother that if she continued to block the bequest, Gina would fight to get the money released in court.

Mr. Mowbry's response had been to go all huffy, and Gina had almost expected him to start quoting that bit in Shakespeare about a child's ingratitude being sharper than a serpent's tooth. Instead he'd hung up.

"If you're as angry and frustrated as you look, your blood pressure is in deep trouble," Nick said.

Gina stared at him, her gaze slowly rising over the long length of his jean-covered legs, over his washboard-flat stomach, over his broad chest covered in a thick navy-blue cotton sweater, over the firm jut of his jaw to come to rest on his wide mouth.

She certainly had been both angry and frustrated, she conceded. But the minute she'd focused on Nick, her anger had evaporated, leaving only frustration. But frustration of a very different sort. Uncertainly she ran the tip of her tongue over her dry lips trying to figure out how her emotions could have shifted so quickly.

"You need to learn to channel your anger."

His voice sounded low and rough in her ears. She swallowed uneasily when she realized that he was suddenly only inches from her. So close that she could feel the heat pouring from his body.

Slowly, as if giving her time to object, he reached out and pulled her up against his large body. She could feel her breasts tightening, her nipples convulsing into tight buds as they collided with his broad chest.

An aching sensation filled her, racing over her nerve endings and pooling in her abdomen, where it tightened, making her feel slightly frantic. As if drawn by some invisible force, her gaze returned to his lips, and a suffocating tension froze the air as her lungs constricted.

Gina wasn't sure whether she bridged the small gap between them or he did, nor did she care. The only thing that mattered to her was that he kiss her. Now. Her need to feel his lips against hers transcended rational thought. Almost as if he shared the same desperate hunger, he lowered his head, and his mouth covered hers with a rough hunger that acted on her like an incredibly powerful aphrodisiac.

Nick traced over her lips with the tip of his tongue, and she instinctively parted them. As if to reward her, his tongue surged inside, sensually exploring the moist interior of her mouth.

Desire slammed through her, making her shudder. Vaguely, as if in the distance, she heard the moan that hummed in her throat, but somehow the sound seemed divorced from her. Her only reality was the feel of his mouth moving against hers. He tasted of coffee and something else. Something far more elusive. Something so elemental, so essentially masculine that it short-circuited her normal inhibitions, and she squirmed against him, mindlessly trying to intensify the erotic sensation.

Her skin felt hot and tight, too tight to contain the feelings rioting through her. She wrapped her arms around him and clung, fighting to stay upright on legs that suddenly felt boneless.

When Nick lifted his head, Gina dragged air into her lungs and brought with it his complicated scent. It set off tiny explosions in the pit of her stomach. Goose bumps popped up on her arms, and an almost painful sense of urgency filled her. She felt as if she were about to go up in flames, and she could hardly wait.

To her immense disappointment, instead of carrying the kiss further, Nick simply stared down at her, his gleaming eyes lingering on her reddened lips.

"Feel better?" his deep voice rasped over her sensitized nerve endings, making her shiver.

For one mad moment Gina considered telling him the truth. That instead of curing her frustration, he'd raised it to unbearable proportions. But a lingering remnant of sanity put a brake on the impulse. If he'd wanted to carry the kiss a step further, he would have. There had been nothing tentative about the way he'd kissed her. He'd known exactly what he was doing and how she'd felt about it, because there had been nothing tentative about her response. And he'd stopped, anyway. Stopped because he'd wanted to. Because he'd had enough. The knowledge stiffened her pride. Clinging to him would only be embarrassing to both of them. She absolutely had to match his level of sophistication. Otherwise he might never kiss her again. And the thought of never getting to feel his lips on hers again made her feel frantic.

Making a supreme effort she stepped back out of his arms and said, "Yes, I feel much better, thank you."

Chapter Eight

"Mygold usually spends his days here," Nick said as he pulled into the parking lot of the Heavenly Repose Funeral Home.

Gina winced when she realized where they were. She didn't want to be here. It brought back too many unhappy memories of the battle with cancer her father had lost.

Reluctantly she opened the truck door and forced herself to get out.

To her surprise, Nick, as if sensing her feelings, caught her hand in his.

Gina swallowed uneasily as his warmth seeped into her fingers and then sped through her veins, heating her blood. What was it about this man that made every hormone she owned go into overdrive the instant he touched her? she wondered in confusion. And, more important, why wasn't he as affected by whatever it was as she was?

Gina shot Nick a quick glance out of the corner of

her eye as they crossed the parking lot. His features wore their normal calm expression. There was nothing on his face to even suggest that he might have found touching her exciting. She stifled a sigh. Skip exciting, she'd settle for any indication at all that he was aware he was touching an available woman.

But she had to be reaching him on some level, she comforted herself, because he'd kissed her. She hadn't forced him to do it. She stole a second look at him, her gaze lingering on his taut jaw. She had the distinct feeling that no one could force Nick Balfour to do anything he didn't want to do.

Her spirits rose slightly. Nick Balfour had kissed her because he wanted to. And kissed her again because he'd enjoyed it the first time. She hugged the thought to herself.

Nick pushed open the door to the funeral home and waited for Gina to enter.

Slowly Gina walked inside, trying to shut out everything but the necessity of getting that police report. It was impossible. The sickly, sweet smell of the white lilies in the vase on the table to the right of the door made her stomach churn, and the funereal quiet beat on her ears.

"You okay?" Nick gave her a sharp look. "You've gone pale."

"I'm fine. I just don't like funeral homes."

"Does sickness bother you?"

"No. If you're sick, you have the hope of getting better, but a funeral home… What was it that Dante said? 'Abandon hope all ye who enter here.'"

Nick reached out and grasped her neck with his left hand and pulled her up against his hard chest, wanting to wipe out the anguish clouding her eyes.

"That was your cue to tell me that death is a welcome release," Gina muttered, fighting an embarrassing urge to burst into tears.

"Sorry, I'm fresh out of platitudes." Nick gently brushed his lips across her trembling mouth.

Gina felt the warmth of his lips flow through her like a benediction. How could his kiss last night have made her want to rip off his clothes, and yet this one made her feel…safe, she finally decided. As if he were a rock that she could lean on.

Mentally she shook her head at the fanciful thought. Not only was she getting maudlin, she was thinking in clichés. No one could make her feel safe. She had to do that for herself.

"What happened to give you such a distaste for funeral homes?" Nick asked.

"My father's death," Gina said tightly.

"Are you an only child?" Nick asked, intensely curious about her.

"Yes, my mother had a difficult pregnancy and could never face trying again," Gina said, for the first time wondering if all her mother's horror stories weren't simply gross exaggerations to justify the fact that she was too selfish to have another child.

"Your father's death must have been rough on your mother?" Nick slipped in another question.

Had it been? Gina tried to remember, but the only specific thing she could actually recall was her mother telling her at the funeral that Gina shouldn't cry because she always looked like a boiled lobster when she did. But who was she to judge the depth of her mother's grief? One thing she did know was that funerals affected people very oddly, and they often said things they normally wouldn't dream of saying.

"They were married for almost thirty years," Gina finally said.

Nick frowned slightly, feeling in his gut that there was something drastically wrong between Gina and her mother. It wasn't so much what she'd said as what she hadn't said. That and the way she'd said it.

But before he could ask any more questions, the sheriff came rushing out of the back of the building.

"Oh, it's just you, Nick," Mygold said, disappointment clear in his face. "I was hoping it might be a customer."

"This concerns your other job," Gina said quickly. All she wanted to do was get her report and get out. Mygold's attitude, on top of everything else, made her feel as if she was dealing with a ghoul. And even though her mind knew that she was being ridiculous, her emotions didn't care.

"My insurance company said they haven't yet received a copy of the police report," Gina said.

"Police report?" Mygold frowned as if he wasn't sure what she was getting at.

"Remember I asked you to send a copy of it by overnight express to my insurance company?"

"Overnight express!" Mygold looked appalled. "Do you have any idea what that costs?"

"Do you have any idea what this delay is costing me?" Gina countered.

Mygold opened his mouth, but before he could say anything, Nick spoke.

"If you try telling us that the wheels of justice grind slowly, Amos, you're going to be in deep trouble," Nick said.

Mygold hastily shut his mouth.

"How about if you give us a copy of the report, and we'll mail it ourselves," Nick said.

"Good idea." Gina seconded it.

Mygold shifted uncomfortably. "Actually, Nick, I haven't gotten it typed up yet. Remember, I told you that Thelma is at her mother's."

"You did report it to the state police, didn't you?" Gina demanded.

"Certainly I did. I just haven't had time to type it yet."

"How about if you make time this morning." Nick's words were phrased as a question, but his tone of voice made it clear that it was an order. "And then when you get it typed, take it down to the post office and overnight it."

Nick pulled his wallet out of his back pocket and, extracting a twenty-dollar bill, handed it to Mygold.

Gina blinked at the speed with which the bill disappeared into Mygold's pocket.

"I'll do it right now," Mygold promised. "And it'll be at the post office before two o'clock, and at the insurance office by tomorrow morning."

"Thank you," Gina muttered.

"See you later." Nick nodded at Mygold and, taking Gina's arm, left.

"Do you think he'll actually do it?" Gina asked once they were back in the truck.

"Yes." Nick swung the truck into the road. "Amos isn't incompetent. He just hates paperwork. Normally he would leave all that to his wife, but with her out of town, his tendency is to procrastinate."

"Thanks for giving him the money to mail it. I'll pay you back when I get my traveler's checks replaced."

Nick simply nodded in response.

"What are you planning on making for dessert tonight?" He changed the subject.

"I hadn't really thought about it. Do you have a preference?"

"Chocolate cake with fudge frosting," he said promptly. "And vanilla ice cream as a chaser."

"You'd do better to take a cholesterol-lowering pill as a chaser," she muttered. "You eat too much junk food."

"My cholesterol is a respectable 125," he said smugly. "I have excellent genes."

Gina's eyes automatically dropped to his lap, lingering on the way his worn jeans lovingly hugged his muscular thighs. Spectacular was more like it, she thought. And she'd love to get inside them. A flush surged under her pale skin, tinting her cheeks pink, and she could feel her breasts growing heavy.

She shifted restlessly, slightly embarrassed by her body's mindless reaction to him, but she refused to apologize even in her own mind for her thoughts. She was a grown woman, and grown women had a perfect right to appreciate male perfection when they found it.

"I hope you thanked your parents for their foresight in passing along such great genetic material," she finally said.

"You can ask them how grateful I am yourself," he said absently as he hurriedly slammed on the brakes to avoid hitting a car that had darted out of the parking lot in front of them.

And when was she going to do that? she wondered. Could Nick be thinking of continuing their relationship once she finally got her car replaced? A starburst of excitement exploded in her, sending her heart rate skyrocketing before common sense doused it. Even if he wanted to, she didn't see how they could. She'd be in school in Illinois, and he'd be here in Massachusetts.

The knowledge left her feeling empty. A feeling she tried to banish by focusing on her goal. She was looking forward to going back to school, she reminded herself. Finishing her degree and getting to work with children was the culmination of a lifelong dream. So why wasn't she feeling more enthusiastic about it? she wondered uneasily. She stole a look at Nick, but he was concentrating on the road.

She wasn't more enthusiastic because for the first time in her life she was absolutely fixated on a man. And that fascination didn't leave room for other, more prosaic emotions such as anticipation of reaching career goals.

"Do I get my cake?" Nick's voice broke into her uneasy thoughts.

"If you're willing to stop at the grocery store. I'm not sure what you have in the line of baking supplies at home."

"Sure, we pass one on the way home."

"And don't forget that we're going to that ballroom dancing lesson tonight," Gina reminded him, praying that the eagerness she was feeling at the thought of getting to spend most of an evening in his arms wasn't showing. It would be humiliating if he were to guess just how enthralled with him she was.

"The dancing lesson was the only thing this evening that sounded interesting other than a lesson on Irish lacemaking. But you don't strike me as a lace person."

He sure could be if she was the one wearing the lace, Nick thought, as his mind conjured up an image of her in a lace nightgown that hugged her slender body from breast to thigh. Black lace, he decided. Very thin black lace so that her gorgeous skin would show through it.

Nick swallowed as he imagined the pale pink of her nipples thrusting against it.

When his body began to enthusiastically react to his thoughts, he made a determined effort to suppress them and failed dismally. The provocative image of Gina lying on his bed, her skin gleaming like a pearl through the black lace, wouldn't be banished.

What the hell was the matter with him? Nick wondered uneasily. He hadn't been this obsessed with a woman since he'd been a teenager. Now he was a mature, responsible surgeon. So why was his body reacting to Gina as if he were still sixteen?

Nick stole a sideways glance at her, his gaze lingering for a fraction of a second on the soft curve of her cheek. Because Gina was different. Not only was she physically gorgeous, but there was something about her personality that appealed to him on a subconscious level he'd never been vulnerable to before. He not only lusted after her, he liked her. He respected her need to be responsible for herself rather than simply accepting the handout he'd originally offered. He admired her desire to teach reading to challenged students. He...

Don't go there, Balfour. He hurriedly cut off his thoughts. She was only here for a few more weeks. Once her insurance check came through, she would be gone. And even if she were willing to stick around a little longer, she was due back at school in Illinois come January. There was no way they could maintain a relationship from that distance.

Although Illinois wasn't the only place that had good teaching schools, he thought. Boston had some of the best in the country. Gina could get a degree from one of them and, if she did that, they could stay in touch. A

dull red scorched his cheekbones at the thought of just
how close he'd like to stay in touch with her.

It was a possibility that was definitely worth exploring. He had a friend who taught at Boston College. He
could ask him to send information about their teaching
program. Then he could show it to Gina and gauge her
reaction. He'd e-mail his friend the minute they got
back, he planned.

One thing was certain, he promised himself as he
pulled into the grocery store parking lot. No matter what
happened in the future he intended to enjoy the present
to the fullest.

Once they were back at the cottage, Nick disappeared
upstairs with a vague mutter about needing to check on
something.

Gina watched him go, wondering if he really did have
something he needed to do or if he was just distancing
himself from her for a while. The fear that she might
have allowed her obsession with him to show momentarily panicked her, but she refused to allow her fear to
grow. Arbitrarily assigning feelings to someone and then
acting as if they were true wasn't just counterproductive,
it was downright stupid.

Gina took a deep breath. She would continue to treat
Nick exactly the way she had been treating him, until
he himself gave her reason to do otherwise. That would
be the mature thing to do, and she was going to be mature about their relationship right up until the day she
drove away from him.

Gina winced as pain tightened her chest, stifling the
breath in her lungs. Getting involved in a relationship
with a man inevitably meant letting go, she told herself.
It was part of the dating process. So why did the thought
of never seeing Nick again make her feel frantic? Prob-

ably because she didn't have any experience to draw on.
The next time she got involved with a man it would be
easier to say goodbye. And the time after that even easier. The thought brought her absolutely no comfort.

"Ready to go?" Nick asked that evening when she
emerged from her bedroom.

"I miscalculated," she said distractedly, her mind
suddenly focused on the way his chinos hugged his muscular thighs. Her gaze lifted, traveling over his flat stomach to linger on the width of his broad shoulders, which
were covered by a pale yellow oxford cloth shirt open
at the neck and a brown Harris tweed jacket. He looked
gorgeous. She just wished she matched him.

"How so?" he asked.

"I forgot that I only had the clothes I bought after my
car was stolen. All I have are jeans," she gestured ruefully at herself. "And I shouldn't be wearing them for
ballroom dancing."

Nick's eyes followed the movement of her hand, his
eyes lingering on the snug fit of her jeans. She sure
shouldn't be wearing them, his hormones agreed with
her. She shouldn't be wearing anything. Nick swallowed
as his mouth suddenly dried under the heat of his imagination. He could hardly wait to get her in his arms. This
evening promised to be the stuff fantasies were made of,
and he had no intention of missing it.

"If you're trying to get out of going, now that I've
taken the trouble to get ready, forget it, woman," he
said. "This was your idea. You can see it through."

Gina took some comfort from the fact that he wanted
to go with her, but it didn't entirely banish her fear of
sticking out like a sore thumb. She hated being conspicuous. Not even the knowledge that her fear stemmed

from her mother's constant belittling references to her height and plainness while she was growing up was enough to banish the feeling.

"Actually I would think that jeans would be better than a skirt," Nick tried to reassure her. "With jeans you'll be able to watch your feet and learn the steps more easily."

"There is that," Gina agreed.

"By the way, I called the sheriff while you were getting ready, and he did send the police report to the insurance company. They should have it before noon tomorrow."

Gina picked her purse up off the kitchen counter and followed him out of the house.

"Did the sheriff say anything else about my car?"

Nick waited until they were in the truck before he answered her.

"Just that the state police haven't found an abandoned car matching yours, so it looks like whoever took it is going to sell it."

"It's too bad they couldn't ransom it off to my insurance company," she said. "It would be a lot less work all around. What makes me so angry is that I have to wait so long to get reimbursed. They have to know that by this point the chances of my car turning up are slim to none. Why won't they simply pay for it and be done with it?"

"Because it's to their advantage to hang on to the money as long as possible. Insurers are by and large cheap bastards!"

Gina blinked under the force of his harsh words. Nick didn't just dislike insurance companies, he loathed them, which was odd. Most people didn't have much of an opinion one way or the other. She hadn't had one herself until this had happened to her and it had been driven home to her that just because one bought insurance to help out in times of crisis didn't mean that the insurance company viewed its role in the same way.

"Did you have a run-in with them when you broke your arm?" she asked curiously.

"No," Nick said, having no intention of telling her that dealing with insurance companies was the bane of his office staff's existence. That would lead to questions he didn't want to answer, and he was sick of giving her evasive answers. He needed to tell her the truth. But not just yet. Not until she knew him a little better.

Maybe he should tell her when the information came that he'd requested on teaching programs in Boston. Then he could work his profession into the conversation. Casually. Something like, oh, by the way, what I really meant when I said I was a technician was that I'm a surgeon. In Boston. He chewed on the inside of his lip as he tried to imagine her response.

She wouldn't care about him being a doctor, he finally decided. Gina was not a woman who was impressed by what a man had or did. What she was going to care about was him deliberately misleading her. She was so straightforward herself, she was going to demand to know why he hadn't just told her from the beginning. And he could hardly tell her that he had been worried that she'd come on to him if she found out about either his profession or his net worth. That made him sound like a conceited jerk.

His fingers tightened around the steering wheel as a sense of frustration filled him. He should never have started this charade in the first place.

Ah, well, he thought as he pulled into the parking lot of the town hall. Hindsight was always twenty-twenty.

He'd worry about it later. Tonight he intended to have fun.

"I wouldn't have expected this many people to be interested in ballroom dancing," Gina whispered to Nick as they entered the hall. "There must be forty people here."

"Mmm." Nick looked around at the gathering. He knew what the appeal for him was, getting to hold Gina in his arms. But he didn't know what the appeal could be for some of the others. Most of the people here appeared to be in their fifties and sixties.

"Exactly what kind of dancing do they do in a ballroom?" Nick asked.

"I haven't a clue," Gina confided. "This is the first ballroom I've ever been in."

Nick chuckled. "You still haven't. This is a gymnasium."

"Lord, deliver me from semanticists," she muttered, starting to get nervous again when she realized that she was the only woman there in pants.

A large, buxom woman called everyone to order and proceeded to take charge in a no-nonsense fashion. After a brief introductory spiel about the joys of ballroom dancing, she had the class members move to the sidelines while she gave a demonstration of the simple waltz they were going to learn that evening.

Gina sighed as she watched the teacher and her partner gracefully dip and sway with the music.

"I wonder how long you have to practice to get that good," she said.

The very pretty brunette standing beside them turned and glanced at Gina. The woman's face was a study in acute boredom, but her expression underwent a miraculous change the minute she saw Nick.

"Nicky!" The woman smiled provocatively at him. "I haven't seen you in ages. I didn't even realize you were…"

"Shellie." Nick hurriedly cut her off before she could say something he didn't want Gina to hear. "How are you?"

"All the better for seeing you, Nicky." Shellie gave him a flirtatious look from beneath her impossibly long lashes.

Nicky! Gina mentally shredded the nickname. Nicky was a child's name, and there was nothing childlike about Nick.

"Gina, I'd like you to meet Shellie Larson."

"Billington." The man Shellie was apparently with corrected him. "Shellie made me the happiest man on earth last month. I'm George, by the way." The man held out his hand to Nick.

"Sorry," Nick said. "I broke my arm."

"Why, Nicky, how frightful for you." Shellie's voice throbbed with emotion. An emotion that struck Gina as phony as a three-dollar bill.

"Sorry, old man," George said. "I didn't see the cast under your jacket.

"We absolutely…" Shellie began only to be interrupted when the teacher called them back to order.

You didn't handle that right, Gina castigated herself, pretending to listen to the teacher's instruction. Instead of standing there like a dummy while Shellie drooled all over Nick, she should have— What? she wondered when her mind remained a blank. Thrown a tantrum? That would hardly have advanced her cause. Men hated scenes. So did most women, come to that. Besides, she had no right to feel possessive about Nick. All that was actually between them was the deal they'd made. Housekeeping for room and board. Hardly the stuff of which great romances were forged. The truth stung.

"Did Shellie bother you?" Nick whispered, catching the slight droop of her lips. "She thinks she's the local belle of the ball."

"She is, of this ball." Gina forced herself to be honest. "She's very pretty."

"And she thinks the fact that she's good-looking excuses her behavior," Nick said acidly. "That poor sucker she has in tow has to be her third husband, maybe her fourth. It's easy to lose track with her."

Gina let her breath out in a sigh of relief. Nick's words were definitely not those of a besotted admirer. Whatever feelings he harbored for Shellie, unrequited love wasn't one of them.

"A foot!" Nick's disbelieving words jerked Gina out of her thoughts.

"Which foot?" Gina hastily glanced toward their instructor, who was standing in the arms of her partner.

"The one that's supposed to be between the two partners while we're learning the waltz. How am I supposed to be able to dance if you're over there, and I'm over here?" he demanded.

"I think we have to work up to something a little more interactive," said the elderly man standing on the other side of Nick.

He'd never last long enough to work up to it, Nick thought in frustration as he maneuvered Gina into the position the teacher was demonstrating. If his level of frustration went any higher, he was liable to grab Gina and kiss her senseless in front of everyone.

He swallowed a chuckle at the thought of the teacher's reaction. Maybe he could pass it off as a variation of the *lambada*.

Chapter Nine

Gina glanced over the kitchen to make sure everything was spotless, peered through the glass cover on the crock pot at the roast cooking for their dinner, and then went looking for Nick.

As if her body were attuned to his on some primitive level she headed for the stairs, somehow knowing he'd be in the upstairs bedroom he used as a study. He was. Gina paused in the open doorway and studied his bent head. The afternoon light streaming in through the dusty window splintered over his body, lovingly caressing his lean cheeks and nestling in his dark hair, giving it a reddish glow.

Her stomach felt as if it were hosting a butterfly convention as her gaze lingered on his long fingers. She shivered as she remembered the pressure of his hands on her back as he'd held her while they'd danced. And when she'd missed a step and stumbled against his hard body... Her heart began to pound against her rib cage.

"Anything wrong?" Nick's question broke into her

thoughts, and she hastily reined in her runaway imagination, making an effort to act normally, even though she was fast coming to the conclusion that around Nick, she didn't know what normal was anymore.

"No, I'm just done cleaning the kitchen, and I wanted to see if you were ready for some exercise. Although…"

Gina took a closer look at his study. The window wasn't the only thing that was dusty. Every available surface was. At least, those surfaces that weren't covered with papers. The place was a mess.

"Are you sure you don't want me to give this room a good cleaning?" she asked.

"Positive." Nick hastily vetoed the idea.

Gina wrinkled her nose. "From the size of some of those piles you don't need a cleaning lady, you need an archeologist. But it's your mess. How about a walk?" she repeated.

"We already did that."

Gina chuckled, and the sound rasped over Nick's nerve endings, pooling in his groin and making him uncomfortably aware of her. Last night had been a big mistake, he realized with the wisdom of hindsight. Holding her in his arms for two hours while they'd danced seemed to have sensitized his body to the point where he was finding it difficult to think of anything but her: the feel of her; the light floral fragrance that always clung to her; the way her eyes had lit with laughter; the way her mouth had tensed with concentration as she counted out the steps of the waltz; and the melodious tone of her voice.

"One is supposed to exercise every day." Gina's voice broke into his thoughts.

"That seems a bit excessive. How about every other day?"

"Every day," she insisted.

"Two days on and one day off," he countered.

"Tell me, do you belong to a union at work?"

"No, why?" he asked in confusion.

"Because you sound like you're auditioning for the part of shop steward."

"I'm simply using logic. Two days out of three would be enough exercise to reap the medical benefits and the free day will encourage me to keep going."

Gina chuckled. "Okay, it's a deal. Two days out of three. Which means we exercise today. Can you come now or are you too busy?"

Gina peered at the papers on his desk, which were stacked beside a couple of thick volumes that looked like reference books. But what could he be researching? she wondered. Much as she wanted to know, snooping was out. Nick would justifiably be furious if he caught her.

Noting her interest in his books and wanting to distract her before she discovered that he'd been reading a medical text, Nick got to his feet and moved toward her. Gina automatically gave way, backing up into the hall. Nick followed her, closing the door behind him.

"Where are we walking to?" Nick asked once he had carefully locked the back door behind them.

"Just out." Gina waved her hand toward the woods that backed onto his property. "Do you really have to lock up so tightly when you leave for a short time?" she asked curiously.

"It's safest," Nick said, not about to tell her that the real reason he did it was because there were always a few fools around who thought that because he was a doctor he kept prescription drugs in the house, and that stealing them would be a good way to turn a quick profit. And too many people in town knew he was a doctor.

The only saving grace in the situation was that they'd known him for so long they almost never referred to his profession.

"I suppose." Gina sighed. "It's a shame, though, that you have to consider that aspect. I mean, it seems so peaceful out here in the woods."

"Crime is everywhere," Nick insisted. "Look at what happened to your car."

"Yes, but that was in town. This is the woods."

"It's still the same world," Nick said. "And a prudent man takes precautions."

Gina chuckled. "Even prudent women do, for all the good it does them. Locking my car probably didn't slow the thief down a bit. But let's talk about something more pleasant."

Nick looked down into her shining face and felt desire zing through him, momentarily clenching his muscles in an agony of wanting. They could talk about sex if she wanted to talk about something more pleasant, he thought. It didn't come much more pleasant than the thought of making love to her.

He hastily chopped off the impulse. He couldn't come on to her too strongly now. He needed to keep everything between them relatively light until she was financially independent of him again. And there was still the problem of her intention of returning to Illinois in January. Maybe this would be a good time to begin laying the groundwork for showing her the material about Boston College once it came.

"Did you start your degree at Illinois?" he asked.

"Yes, I was at the main campus in Champaign-Urbana until my father was diagnosed with lung cancer." Gina's voice tightened with remembered pain.

"And the truly frustrating thing was that he had never smoked in his life."

Wanting only to ease the pain he could see in her face, Nick reached out and gave her a quick hug. "One of the hardest lessons anyone has to learn is that life isn't fair."

Gina released her breath in a long sigh. For some reason his casual gesture of sympathy made her feel much better.

"So you decided to go back to Illinois to finish your degree?" Nick asked when she remained silent.

"Yes, I needed to take control of my life again."

"A terminal illness can make you feel totally out of control," Nick agreed.

It wasn't her father's illness that had made her feel like that, Gina thought. It was her mother's manipulation.

"I like Illinois. It…" Gina broke off as she suddenly remembered that she might not be returning to school in January. The university had been very accommodating about allowing her to enroll for the second semester even though she had missed the cutoff date for applying. But she doubted that their accommodation would include waiting indefinitely for their money. It all depended on how long her mother could legally tie up her father's bequest.

"Maybe you ought to expand your horizons," Nick cautiously offered.

Gina glanced around the open woods and said, "My horizons are pretty broad at the moment."

"I meant schoolwise. Have you considered finishing your degree somewhere else?"

Gina's heart stopped beating for a second and then began a frantic rhythm that made her feel light-headed. Could he want her to finish her degree around here?

Could he like her enough as a woman to ask her to stay here, where they could continue to see each other?

"Boston has some really great schools," Nick's next words sliced her hope out from underneath her, plunging her into a pit of pain. He didn't want her to stay near him. He was just making conversation. Boston was at least four hours away.

"Every university I've ever run across demands you take two years of courses at their school. So if I transferred, I'd lose almost a whole year's work." And money, she added. And at the moment, the money was of far greater importance than the time.

"True," Nick murmured, "but maybe you could use some of the extra class work to apply toward your master's. You are going to get your master's, aren't you?"

"Oh, yes. But I was going to do it part-time while I taught. I've gotten rather attached to eating."

Nick frowned. He wanted to tell her that he would take care of her bills, but he didn't dare. For one thing he didn't think she'd accept. For another he didn't want to blow his cover yet. It was enough that he had planted the idea of a different school, he told himself. He'd drop it for now, and then when the literature from Boston College came, he'd casually introduce the subject again.

"How far are we walking today?" Nick asked.

Gina checked her watch. "Let's go another ten minutes, and then we'll turn back. Although I think we ought to pick up our pace a little. I'm not sure if the fact that the terrain is rough equals not being able to walk at a brisk pace."

"What is a brisk pace?" Nick asked.

"The article I read didn't say," she admitted. "I guess it means fast."

"And how fast is fast? Fast enough to make you

breathless? Fast enough to tire you out? Fast enough to—'' Nick broke off as Gina slipped on the edge of the pathway and started to slide down the steep embankment toward the shallow stream below.

She jerked backward to try to regain her balance and fell. With a muttered imprecation, she slid down the hill on her rear and landed in the stream with a splash.

Nick hastily followed her down. Plucking her out of the water, he set her on her feet.

''Fast enough to break your neck?'' he finished his original question.

''I didn't break anything. Besides, it's hardly my fault that the edge of the gully crumbled,'' she muttered, then shivered as the icy water soaked through her jeans.

''No, but it will be your fault if you catch cold hanging around in wet clothes. Come on.'' He took her arm and hauled her back up the incline. ''Home and a hot bath for you.''

When she reached the path a sharp gust of wind attacked her, and she shuddered from the cold.

''Maybe you should take them off.'' Nick eyed her jeans consideringly. ''You could use my sweater to dry off and then…''

''No.'' Gina flatly refused. No way was she going to strip down to her underwear in front of him. She simply didn't have the kind of self-confidence to carry that off. Not with skinny legs and plain white cotton panties. She'd be more likely to inspire amusement in a man than uncontrollable lust.

Which is what she wanted to inspire in Nick, she admitted on a burst of honesty. She wanted him to take one look at her and not be able to keep his hands off her. She wanted him to be consumed with desire. She wanted…the moon, she conceded. A femme fatale she wasn't. Heck, she not only wasn't fatal to men, she wasn't even capable of delivering a glancing blow.

The truth made her wince.

"Hurry up." Nick grabbed her arm and hurried her along.

Gina went, far more interested in the feel of his fingers wrapped around her arm than the fact that her shoes squished with every step she took and her jeans chafed the tender skin of her inner thighs.

To her dismay, once they were on level ground he let go of her arm, and she felt bereft. As if she'd lost her anchor. Or her mind! Nick was nothing more than a friend. That was all. So what if he'd kissed her a couple of times. Friends kissed all the time. It didn't mean a thing. She stole a quick glance at Nick. It especially didn't mean a thing with a handsome man like Nick.

"Go take a hot shower while I make a pot of coffee," Nick ordered her once they reached the back porch. "I don't want you coming down with something."

How about someone? Gina thought. She'd love to come down with him. Preferably on the bed. What would he look like without his clothes? She stole a covert glance at him as he unlocked the door. Would he have the same inky black hair on his chest as he had on his head? What would it feel like if she were to press herself against his hair-covered chest?

Gina swallowed as she felt the tips of her breasts tightening to pebble hardness. Her breathing shortened, and a flush swept over her cheeks.

Nick unlocked the door, pushed it open and then turned to her.

"Damn! You're flushed," he bit out.

"I won't catch anything," Gina said, grateful he was blaming her dunking for her physical reaction. It would

be humiliating in the extreme if he realized she had sunk
to the level where all she had to do was to look at him
to be turned on. "I read once that getting wet or chilled
doesn't cause illness," she added for good measure.

"That's true as far as it goes. But getting chilled low-
ers the body's resistance and, if you happen to have any
germs lurking in your system, it makes it easier for them
to attack."

Not a problem, Gina thought. In order to attack, the
germs would first have to get her body's attention off
Nick and that would be no small feat.

"Go on." Nick gave her a gentle push toward her
bedroom.

Gina went.

Ten minutes later she was clean, dry and warm. She
entered the kitchen again to find Nick waiting. He gave
her a quick, assessing look that by no stretch of the
imagination could be called loverlike, and then poured
her a cup of coffee.

"Here, drink this. How do you feel?"

"Clean." She grinned at him. "And wiser. Next time
we go walking I'll stay away from the edge of the path."

"Maybe we ought to take up another kind of exercise?" He eyed her thoughtfully. He knew what kind of
exercise he'd like to introduce her to, he thought. Hadn't
he read somewhere that making love burned up four
hundred calories? He'd bet that making love to her
would burn a whole lot more than that. He shifted restlessly as his skin felt too tight to contain his body. Hell,
all he had to do was look at Gina and his body temperature shot up. If he ever got to make love to her, the
resulting conflagration would probably consume them
both.

He couldn't make love to her now, he reasoned with

his desire. But he could if she were to finish her degree in Boston. Then they'd be meeting as equals. She wouldn't be dependent on him for anything.

If she were in Boston, he could spend time with her. It wouldn't be hard to cut back a little on his work. Maybe free up a few evenings and the occasional weekend. They could…

"I think I'll call the traveler's check people again." Gina's words broke into his plans. "Maybe I'll get lucky, and the supervisor will have finally shown up."

Putting her empty coffee cup on the counter, Gina mentally gathered her inner resources to do battle with the bureaucrats.

To her surprise it wasn't a battle. The person who'd answered the phone pulled her file up immediately and put her right through to the supervisor. The supervisor apologized for the delay, assured Gina the checks would be reissued and air-expressed to her that afternoon.

Gina had put down the phone with a feeling of shock.

"What's wrong?" Nick asked.

"I just ran across the first competent, reasonable person in this whole mess," she said in surprise. "Not only that, but he resisted the impulse to tell me I should have kept the check numbers in a safe place. He's going to express the replacement checks to me. They should be here tomorrow morning sometime."

"The law of averages suggests that one of them should know what they're doing," Nick said. "Want to go out to dinner to celebrate?"

Gina briefly weighed eating out among a crowd of people against staying at home here with just the two of them, and opted for alone. Not only that but she didn't feel comfortable letting him spend money on her when it was clear he didn't have all that much.

"Another time." She tried to sound causal. "I've already got the roast cooking."

"Then we can have the rest of that chocolate cake for dessert," he said.

"Man does not live by chocolate alone."

He grinned at her. "Maybe not, but it would sure be fun to try sometime. If you should…"

The phone rang, and Nick automatically answered it with a crisp, "Balfour."

Gina eyed him uncertainly. For a second there, Nick had sounded like someone else. Someone authoritative. Someone…

"It's for you." Nick handed her the phone. "A man."

For her? A man? Gina stared blankly down at the black receiver he was holding out to her as she tried to figure out what man would be calling her. He would have recognized the sheriff's voice. Maybe it was about the insurance? A spurt of excitement shot through her, and then was quickly drowned as she realized that once her car was replaced she would no longer have any excuse to stay here. Although she might be able to drag out buying a replacement car for weeks. Cheered by the thought, she reached for the phone.

"Hello?" she said. "This is Gina Tessereck."

"Gina, this is Reverend Milsom."

"Oh?" Gina said cautiously. She wasn't fond of the Reverend Milsom or of his church. As far as she was concerned, they were a bunch of smugly self-centered hypocrites who felt that everyone who thought the way they did was great and everyone who didn't was going straight to hell without even passing go.

The only reason Gina had continued to attend his church was that her mother went and demanded Gina drive her. The few times Gina had suggested simply dropping her mother off for services and picking her up later, her mother had burst into tears.

She had no idea why the minister would want to talk to her. She frowned slightly. And for that matter, how had he gotten her number? Unfortunately, she wasn't left in doubt for long.

"I just got back from visiting your mother," Reverend Milsom said. "And I can't begin to tell you how shocked I am."

"But you're going to try, anyway." The irreverent comment slipped out before Gina could stop it.

"This is not a matter of levity. The Bible instructs us to honor our mother and our father, and for you to simply go off and leave your mother in her condition is a mortal sin."

Gina glanced over at Nick. To her relief he was leafing through a stack of videos on the table, not paying any attention to her conversation.

"There is nothing wrong with her condition," Gina said. "In fact, it would improve tremendously if she were to do something novel such as get a part-time job."

"You are putting your immortal soul in danger by your callous disregard for your mother's welfare. You have to come home immediately," he demanded.

"Not this side of hell," Gina said softly and hung up the phone. Her surge of satisfaction was quickly superseded by a feeling of bleakness at her mother's duplicity. How could any mother treat her daughter the way hers was doing?

Look at the bright side, she told herself. At least you've got a complete set of blueprints on how not to raise a child. The thought brought her no comfort.

"Problems?" Nick watched the expressive emotions

flickering across her face. Whoever that sanctimonious voice had belonged to had upset her. Badly.

Taking a deep breath, she forced a wavering smile. "No, just a minor annoyance. Nothing to worry about."

A minor annoyance wouldn't make her look as if she'd just lost her last friend, Nick thought grimly, but there was no way he could force her confidence, and until she was ready to confide in him, he would have to play a waiting game.

Picking up one of the videos, he headed toward the stairs. "I'll be upstairs if you should need me."

Gina watched him leave the room and then went into the kitchen and poured herself a second cup of coffee as she ordered her insides to stop shaking. Why wouldn't her mother leave her alone! She was a relatively young woman. Why didn't she live her own life?

Gina sniffed back an impulse to burst into tears. If she was going to demand answers to impossible questions, she might as well ask why she hadn't been born beautiful and sexy.

Life, as they were forever telling you, was a bitch, she thought glumly.

But not all of it, she mentally countered the saying. Right at the moment parts of her life were definitely worth savoring. And the best part was upstairs working on whatever it was he worked on in his study.

Feeling much better, she started to peel the potatoes for dinner.

Chapter Ten

Gina looked from the slightly bent candles she held in her hand to the kitchen table, which she had set for dinner. She squinted into the middle distance as she tried to imagine what Nick would look like in candlelight.

Fantastic, she decided as an image of him with the flickering light reflecting off his high cheekbones formed in her mind. Actually Nick would look fantastic in any kind of light. He had the kind of bone structure that transcended time. He'd still be a striking looking man when he was ninety.

Not that she'd be here to see it, she thought with a feeling of sadness that caught her off guard. She'd met him at the wrong time in her life for him to be anything other than a temporary diversion. Their embryonic relationship would never survive her living in the Midwest while he was in Massachusetts. Not that he had shown any signs that he even wanted to try to maintain contact once she left. She winced as she remembered his casual comment about Boston's schools. Boston might be closer to him than Illinois, but it was still too far to carry on a romance.

Unfortunately, while her mind might know that her relationship was doomed, her body didn't care. It wanted Nick. Wanted his arms around her. Wanted to feel the hard pressure of his mouth against hers. Wanted to feel the heavy weight of his body pressing down on hers.

She'd just have to keep her mind in control, she told herself. And the only way to do that was to stay focused on the fact that, while she might want him with a craving that bordered on the addictive, she'd seen no sign that he felt the same way. She might not have a great deal of experience with men, but common sense told her that if he wanted to make love to her, he would have let her know. And he hadn't. All he'd done was kiss her a few times.

Gina sighed as she put the candles back in the pantry where she'd found them. Candlelight was out. She didn't need her vision blurred any more than it was.

Checking to make sure everything was ready for dinner, Gina hurried to the bottom of the stairs and called to Nick. She didn't get an answer.

Assuming he had the door closed and couldn't hear her, she hurried up the stairs and headed toward the end bedroom, which Nick used as a study.

To her surprise the door was standing wide-open, and she peered inside.

Nick was watching a video on the small television he had on his desk with an intentness that shut out distractions.

Frowning, she moved into the room as she tried to make sense of what she was seeing on the screen. Probably some kind of horror film, she thought, because that looked like...

A gasp of horror escaped when she realized exactly what she was looking at. Two hands were lifting the heart of a child out of its chest. Gina gulped as nausea swirled through her. The only thing missing was blood.

Nick glanced over his shoulder as the strangled sound she made penetrated his intense concentration, and he hurriedly clicked off the television.

"Is dinner ready?" he asked.

"Dinner?" Gina repeated as if it were a foreign word and she had no clue as to its meaning. "How can you even think of eating after seeing that…" She waved impotently at the now-blank screen.

Damn! Nick thought. Now what did he do? He could lie, provided he could come up with a plausible one, or he could tell her the truth and risk spoiling what had been some of the best days of his life.

Nick studied her pale face and jettisoned the idea of lying. He might have been able to lie to her when he had first met her, but he couldn't bring himself to do it now. Because he loved her. The appalling thought slammed through his mind with the force of a jackhammer. How could he have been so stupid as to fall in love with her? He knew the problems it would cause. He didn't have time to devote to a permanent relationship. He already had a demanding mistress—surgery.

Although maybe he didn't. His eyes dropped to the cast on his arm, and a feeling of bleak despair filled him. He might never regain the dexterity needed to operate again. Then what would he have? Nothing. Not a damn thing that meant anything to him. The answer filled him with mind-numbing pain.

"Nick?"

Hurriedly he shoved both his unwelcome discovery and his fears for the future to the back of his mind. He'd worry about them later. For now Gina had asked a question that he had to answer and, if the truth changed things between them, then he'd add that problem to the list to be dealt with later. At the rate his list was growing, he'd be years straightening it out, he thought wryly.

"It's not an entertainment film," he said. "It's a demonstration video of a new technique being used in Switzerland."

"Technique?" Gina queried.

"Operating technique for heart transplants. It's getting good results."

"Good results?" Gina parroted. "You mean you're interested in watching operations?" she tried to make sense of what he was telling her.

"In a way." Nick took a deep breath and blurted out, "I am a thoracic surgeon, and I'm always interested in improving my skills."

Gina frowned. "A surgeon? But you said you were a technician."

"I am. I simply use a scalpel as my tool of choice."

Gina chewed on her lower lip as she tried to fit what she had just learned into what she already knew about Nick. It was easy. She had no trouble picturing him as a doctor. He certainly had the intelligence. And he projected a calm that must be very soothing to his patients.

But why had he lied to her in the first place? Not directly, she conceded, but he knew she'd drawn the conclusion that he was a factory worker. The conclusion he'd wanted her to draw. Could he have realized how attracted she'd been to him and wanted to put her off by claiming a less prestigious profession? But that didn't really make any sense. If he'd been worried she might try to cling to him, he would never have invited her into his home.

"Why didn't you tell me the truth in the beginning?" she asked, needing to know.

"Because most women tend to treat me differently once they find out I'm a doctor."

Gina studied him for a minute and then asked, "How?"

Nick shifted uneasily, afraid he was going to sound like an egomaniac.

"When some of them find out about my profession, they see a husband who can provide them with a luxurious lifestyle. And that's before they even find out about the trust fund my grandfather left me," he said, deciding to tell her everything at once and get it over with.

"And those who aren't trying to marry my bank balance invariably wind up giving me their physical symptoms and asking me to diagnose them on the spot," he added when she didn't say anything.

"You're perfectly safe from me," her pride demanded she tell him. "I don't need some man to pay my bills, and I am perfectly healthy."

Cautiously, Gina probed her feelings about his claiming to have been just a technician and found that it didn't bother her. He'd misled her before he'd known her. But now that he knew her as a person, he was willing to risk telling her the truth. And he hadn't had to. She doubted that she would ever have known what he did for a living if he had kept quiet. His telling her the truth was a step forward in their relationship. At least, she hoped it was.

To Nick's surprise, Gina's words didn't reassure him. They made him mad. He didn't want her to write him off as unnecessary. He wanted her to… To do what? Throw herself in his arms and declare undying love?

Yes, he admitted. That was exactly what he wanted her to do. Even though he knew it would create big problems in both their lives—problems that could only be solved by major compromises on both sides—he still wanted her to say she loved him.

But just because she didn't love him at the moment didn't mean that she might not come to love him later, he consoled himself. She already responded to him physically. With a little encouragement...

"I know you aren't after my money," he finally said.

"Actually, that's not precisely true," she said. "Now that I know you aren't broke, I'd like to separate you from about five hundred dollars of it in the interest of indigestion."

"What indigestion?"

"The indigestion you're going to get when you eat the burned parts from the muffins I made for dinner because the temperature gauge in the oven of that antique you euphemistically call a stove doesn't work."

"I don't cook much," he said.

"But I do."

"Point taken. One new stove. Is there anything else?"

Gina briefly debated telling him to pick up a couple of gallons of paint while he was at it so that she could cover the appalling color in the living room, but decided not to. He might think she was angling to stay longer if she started redecorating his house. There was no way she was going to put herself in the same category as the women who chased him.

"No, the stove will be fine. Actually, I came to tell you that dinner was ready."

"Good, I'm starved."

Gina cast a quick glance at the blank television screen and shuddered. Nick must have a cast-iron stomach, she thought, as she followed him downstairs.

"It looks delicious," Nick said, once they were seated at the table.

"Wait a minute."

Nick paused in the act of spreading butter on his muffin. "Why?" He peered down at it, not seeming to notice the burned bottom.

"Not that. I just thought of something. If you're a doctor, why don't you exercise?"

"No time."

"But a doctor should know better," she insisted.

"So should you, but you don't exercise, either," Nick pointed out as he slathered strawberry jam on his muffin.

"Yes, well... Do you normally practice around here?" she asked, to change the subject.

"No, this really is just my family's summer cottage. I simply came here to wait it out while my arm healed."

Encouraged by the way he was answering her questions, Gina decided to ask a few more while she had the chance.

"Where do you practice?"

"In Boston."

And Boston was where the school with the good education department he'd been telling her about was located, Gina remembered. Which meant what exactly? Had he simply been bragging about one of his hometown schools, or could it possibly mean that he wanted to continue seeing her after she left here and knew it would be easier if they were both in the same city?

Excitement exploded in her chest, momentarily making her feel light-headed. It was possible. But not probable. She tried to put a brake on her elation. But how was she supposed to find out? And even if she did discover that he wanted her in Boston so they could continue to see each other, was she willing to start over at a new school and add almost a year to the time it was going to take her to finish?

Gina surreptitiously studied Nick's dark features, her eyes lingering on his lips. The sudden surge of desire that speared through her caught her off guard, and she shifted in her seat in dismay. All she had to do was to look at the man and her body went on red alert. But why? She chased the question around her mind, trying to come up with an answer. Why should this one man affect her so profoundly?

Granted he was handsome, but she'd known more handsome men who'd left her cold. She also liked his sharp intelligence and his willingness to try new things. For a moment her thoughts were sidetracked as she wondered if that willingness to embrace new things extended to bed. The very thought of what kind of lover he might be sent a hectic flush over her cheeks, and she hurriedly took a drink of water.

"These muffins aren't at all bad," Nick said as he helped himself to a second one.

"Thanks, I read somewhere that charcoal is good for your digestive tract."

"Then maybe I shouldn't toss out the old stove."

"Allow me to rephrase that, I've heard that a *little* charcoal is good for your digestive tract."

He grinned. "Why is it there's always a catch?"

And what was the catch with Nick? Gina wondered. Her subconscious immediately supplied the answer. The catch was that he could break her heart and never even know it. Because she loved him, the totally unexpected revelation poured through her mind with the shocking awareness of an icy bath.

How could she have done something so monumentally stupid as to fall in love with a man who had been brutally blunt about what he thought of women chasing him? For that matter when had she done it? When had lust and liking tipped over into a love that threatened her peace of mind? She didn't know. All she knew for certain was that she was in deep trouble.

"Are you okay?" Nick eyed her narrowly. "You didn't come down with something from that dip in the creek, did you? Does anything hurt?"

Just my common sense, she thought grimly.

"I'm fine. I never get sick." She forced a casual smile, wishing her moment of self-enlightenment had come when she'd been alone so that she could have had time to muster her defenses.

"Wait until you start teaching," he said. "The wife of a friend of mine got a job teaching kindergarten a few years back, and she caught every bug going the first year. Although after that she seemed to build up some immunity."

"An occupational hazard." Gina gratefully latched on to the impersonal subject, wondering how long it would take her to test the theory. If her mother continued to block her legacy, it could be years before she was able to finish her degree. And given her mother's behavior in the past, it was highly unlikely that she'd drop the suit simply because it was in Gina's best interests.

A feeling of sadness swept over her making her want to cry. Her father had been the one who had loved her. The one who had never been too busy to listen to her childish enthusiasm. Looking back on it, Gina realized that her mother had never been able to even momentarily cede center stage to anyone, even to her own daughter.

Gina jumped as Nick put his hand over her clenched fist. The tingling warmth of his fingers seeped into her rigid flesh, dislodging her somber thoughts.

"Why so solemn?" he asked.

"I was just thinking about my father."

"What was he like?" Nick removed his hand, and Gina momentarily felt deprived.

"A really great person," she muttered, not wanting to discuss her father because that would lead to her mother, and she most emphatically didn't want to try to explain her mother to Nick. He might think there was something lacking in Gina herself if her own mother couldn't love her.

Nick bit back a sense of impotent frustration at her refusal to share her thoughts with him. He wanted to take her in his arms and kiss the lost, unhappy look off her face. He wanted to assure her that she wasn't alone. That he was there for her. That he loved her. But he'd seen no sign that she would welcome such a declaration from him. On the contrary, she kept talking about returning to Illinois. That certainly didn't sound like someone who would be willing to compromise and finish up her degree in Boston. From everything he could tell, she only wanted his friendship. She hadn't even gotten mad that he'd lied to her about his profession. Of course, she might also have realized that he might not be a surgeon when this was all over.

He glanced down at his cast in bitter anguish. If there had been nerve damage…

"Does your arm hurt?" Gina shivered at the pain she could see etched in his face.

"No," he said flatly.

"When does your cast come off?" she risked another question in the face of his uncompromising negative.

"A couple of weeks. Then I'll have an X ray, and Sam'll assess the healing."

"Sam?"

"The orthopedist who wired the bone back together."

Wired it back together? Gina weighed his words. That didn't sound like a simple fracture to her.

"How did you break it?"

"I didn't exactly break it," he said.

A chill iced Gina's skin at his words. Did he have some kind of degenerative disease that made his bones snap?

"Exactly what happened?" Fear sharpened her voice.

"The bone was shattered by a bullet."

"A bullet!" Gina eyed him in horror. "Where were you that you got shot?"

"In the hospital emergency room assessing the condition of an accident victim." Nick ran his fingers through his hair in remembered frustration. "They have metal detectors at the entrances, which are supposed to prevent people from bringing in weapons. But that night the guard had turned them off because they kept going off on false alarms and disturbing everyone. So when some kids brought in their buddy who was strung out on drugs, the fact that he was carrying a 9 mm automatic didn't register."

"Good Lord!" Gina shivered at the scenario he'd just described.

"Yes. Anyway, when the nurse tried to treat him, the kid thought he was being attacked and shot her. I was in the next cubicle with the accident victim."

"And you tried to take the gun away from him," Gina had no trouble imagining what happened.

"I had no choice. The nurse was lying on the floor hemorrhaging. She clearly needed immediate medical attention, and who knew who else the guy might shoot. He wasn't exactly rational." A grim smile tightened

Nick's lips. "Or a good shot. He yelled he was going to blow my head off, but he only hit my arm."

Gina blindly grasped his hand, wanting the comfort of his touch.

"You could have been killed," she whispered, horrified at the thought that she could have lived her entire life and never have known him. It would have been like being color-blind and never realizing that there was a whole world of rich color out there to savor.

"I hope they took that guard out and dropped him down a deep dark hole, and then covered it up after him!" she snapped. "He didn't want to be bothered, and as a result you and a nurse got shot. Was she okay?"

"She will be eventually, although she swears she'll never work in an emergency room again."

"I don't blame her." Gina shuddered. "I never thought of hospitals as dangerous places before."

"They aren't usually. But what happened means that I may not ever again have the manual dexterity necessary to operate," he said, wanting to make sure she understood that his days as an eminent surgeon could well be over. "While the bone appears to be knitting well, it's impossible to tell how much nerve and muscle damage there was. That won't become apparent until I start physical therapy."

Gina winced at his expression. He looked grim and slightly frantic. But what could she say? "Gee, that's too bad" didn't quite cover it. His problems made her concern about the delay of finishing her degree seem petty. Eventually she would be able to teach. Nick had no such assurance he'd ever operate again.

"Only time will give you the answer, and the waiting must be hell," she finally said.

"Not so much since you showed up," he said honestly. "You were right about my not having any outside interests to fall back on to take my mind off my worries. I'd let myself become totally immersed in my work."

Gina felt a glow of happiness at his words. "But we still haven't figured out what interests you," she said to distract his somber thoughts.

"Is there anything listed in the paper for tonight?" he asked, eagerly grasping at the change of subject.

"Only choir practice at the Methodist church. They're looking for new members." She eyed him questioningly.

"Not of my caliber," he said emphatically. "I couldn't carry a tune to save my life."

"They aren't in a position to complain."

"Why not?" he asked curiously.

"Because the Bible says that we are to make a joyful noise unto the Lord. It didn't say anything about doing it in tune."

"I don't care who has the moral high ground. I hate it when the people around me cringe," he said. "What about tomorrow?"

"There is a big flea market in Vinton. We could go there."

"With a view to doing what?"

"You might take up collecting."

Nick eyed her bright expression. The only thing he wanted to collect was her. And as soon as possible, before someone else snapped her up. On the other hand, even if he didn't have the slightest desire to poke through anyone else's junk, he'd still enjoy spending the day with her.

"You're on," he agreed. "The flea market it is."

Chapter Eleven

"Maybe what you need is a lawyer?" Nick said as Gina returned to the kitchen the following morning after her daily phone call to the insurance company.

"A lawyer would charge me more than the car is worth. And I really don't have anywhere specific I have to be before next month," she said.

"Then why do you keep calling them?" Nick asked, trying to figure out what her motivation was. He'd thought she was happy here with him, but if she was, then why did she keep trying to hurry up the insurance company?

"It's the principle of the thing," she muttered, giving him part of the reason. The other reason was so that Nick wouldn't suspect just how much she enjoyed being here with him. How much she was looking forward to spending the next couple of weeks with him. For the first time in her adult life, her dream of teaching had taken a backseat. Her feelings for Nick were more important. A fact that worried her when she allowed herself to think about it.

Nick eyed her tense features and thought better of offering to pay the lawyer's fees. Gina was very independent. Offering her money would undoubtedly upset her. And he didn't want to upset her. He wanted to make love to her. His eyes lingered on her tightly compressed lips. He wanted to press his own against them. He wanted to apply pressure until they parted. He wanted to taste her. He wanted to make love to her with a desire that was fast becoming an obsession.

And he would, he promised himself. But he couldn't rush it. He didn't want Gina for a quick affair. He wanted her in his life on a permanent basis. He wanted to see her across the table from him every morning and to go to bed with her every night for the rest of his life. He wanted to marry her. And the only way he had even a hope of doing that was by playing a waiting game. And the first move in the game had to be to convince her that Illinois wasn't the only place where she could finish her degree. That Boston would do just as well.

Once she accepted that, then he could risk moving their relationship to a more intimate level. Until then, though, he had to keep everything casually friendly between them.

"Allow me to give you a news flash," Nick said. "Your pursuit of a principle is going to give you high blood pressure."

"Ha! You're a great one to talk. Your lack of outside interests is far more likely to raise your blood pressure than me bashing my head up against a bureaucratic wall."

Nick took a swallow of his cooling coffee and said, "I've been thinking about that, and I do have a hobby."

Gina eyed him dubiously. "What's that?"

"Medicine."

"That's not a hobby, that's your profession." And from the sound of it his whole life, Gina thought unhappily. There seemed to be no place in his life for a relationship with a woman. The thought depressed her.

Nick's features tightened as the fears that were never far below the surface of his mind erupted. "Surgery might not be either my hobby or my profession once my cast comes off."

Gina winced at the despair she could see etched on his face. Instinctively she reached out and placed her fingers over his hand.

Nick felt the touch of her fingers against his skin like a brand. Tiny pinpricks of sensation raced along his nerve endings, making him feel edgy and intensely aware of her.

"I wish there was something I could say to make you feel better." Her frustration was clear in her voice.

"Words aren't going to make any difference," Nick said bleakly. But actions might, he thought as his eyes lingered on her soft pink lips. Making love to her would make him forget his fears. At least for a while.

Gina heaved a sigh. "You're right, of course," she said. "There's nothing to do but to wait it out. What does the doctor say about your chances?"

"Sam said that I should have enough flexibility to handle most everyday tasks."

"And surgery involves more than simply normal flexibility?" she said.

"A hell of a lot more! And it can't be faked. People's lives depend on the surgeon's skill. I don't know what I'm going to do if…"

He got to his feet, jerked there by the force of his

anguish, and stalked over to the counter. Gina watched as he rubbed the back of his neck with his left hand, and she found herself wanting to be the one to touch him. To run her fingers through his silky soft hair. To absorb the heat flowing off his smooth skin. To somehow ease his almost palatable despair. But she didn't dare. If she tried to step outside the parameters of the friendly relationship he'd established, she might well wreck the companionship they were presently sharing, and she'd be left with nothing.

Nick swung around and faced her. "Aren't you going to tell me that I can still practice medicine even if I can't operate?"

Gina ran the tip of her tongue over her dry lips and tried to judge his mood. Volatile, she decided. Perhaps her best response would be the truth combined with common sense. He was far too smart to be taken in by platitudes, and he didn't want pity. She was as sure of that as she was of her own name.

"You don't need me to tell you that. You already know it, and if you found any comfort in the fact, you wouldn't be so worried about how your arm is going to heal." She forced herself to sound matter-of-fact.

"Do you think I'm being childish?" The question seemed wrenched from him.

"Because you're worried that you might lose everything you've worked for?" she said incredulously. "You wouldn't be much of a surgeon if you didn't feel that it was the most important branch of medicine."

Nick felt something relax inside him at her words. "But surgery isn't the only one," he forced himself to repeat what all his colleagues at the hospital had kept telling him, until he'd finally retreated to the cottage to get away from their well-meant but useless reassurances.

"True," she agreed. "I guess it would be like if I couldn't get a job as a reading instructor and had to settle for teaching high school English. It wouldn't be the age group I wanted or the subject I was fascinated with."

"Would you do it?"

"Yes," she said honestly. "It would still be teaching."

"The problem is that I'm not particularly interested in any other branch of medicine," he admitted.

"I think if I were a doctor I'd like to be an obstetrician," she said. "Births are such happy events."

Nick looked at her and his mind instantly supplied an image of Gina pregnant. Of her slim body softly rounded with a baby. His baby. Desire slammed through him, and he gritted his teeth to force it down.

"Obstetrics is ninety-nine percent routine and one percent sheer terror," he said, quoting a colleague of his.

Gina wrinkled her nose. "I kind of like routine. Ad-libbing on the fly is not my thing."

Deciding it was time to change the subject, she said, "We need to leave. The flea market opens at one."

"What made you think of collecting as a hobby?" he asked.

"I got the idea from a *Jeeves and Wooster* episode I saw on A&E a while back. The one where the old man collected Georgian silver."

Nick thought of all the silver his grandmother had collected, which now was stored in bank vaults. He didn't know what time period she'd specialized in, but he did know that caring for silver was a time-consuming, messy chore that didn't appeal to him in the slightest.

"You expect to find silver at a flea market?" he asked curiously.

"Don't be deliberately obtuse."

"How about inadvertently?" Nick asked, fascinated by the way she had no hesitation slapping him down. She was the only person he knew who did it. Most people tiptoed around him, either awed by his skill with a scalpel or by the amount of money he had. Gina wasn't impressed by either. She simply treated him like a friend. It was a refreshing change. Now if he could just get her to treat him like a lover, it would be perfect.

"You have to delve into all the possibilities before you can decide what you want to collect," she said. "And a flea market should offer lots of possibilities. The paper said there were over 150 stalls."

And it would take most of the afternoon to examine them, he realized. Spending the day with Gina promised to be infinitely more enjoyable than staying home and worrying about his arm.

"I'm game," he said. "Where exactly is this flea market?"

"At the armory in Vinton." Gina felt her spirits rise. Suddenly the day seemed brighter, its edges more sharply defined.

"I'll get my purse and meet you at the front door," she said.

To Gina's surprise, it wasn't Nick who was fascinated by the flea market. It was she.

"Look at that," she said as they entered the huge armory.

Nick glanced around the crowded space. "Look at what?"

"Books! Used books." She pointed to the row of tables piled high with paperbacks set up to the right of the entrance.

"Let's see what they've got." She headed toward the tables.

Nick watched as she began to eagerly sift through the dusty volumes.

"Are you allergic to anything?" he asked.

"No," she said absently as she pulled a copy of Agatha Christie's *The Mystery at Styles* out of the stack. "Why?"

"Because some of these books have a distinct odor of moldy basement about them."

"Just ignore those. There are plenty of others." Gina chortled with glee when she discovered a second Agatha Christie mystery novel she hadn't read.

Nick barely glanced at the piles of books. He was too fascinated by Gina's absorbed features as she carefully combed through them.

It was an hour before she was willing to call it quits. By then she had a sizable cardboard box filled with paperbacks.

"Didn't you find anything?" she suddenly seemed to realize that he was the one who was supposed to be collecting things.

"Yes, a copy of an Umberto Eco book I hadn't read."

Gina looked from the overflowing box of books at her feet to the slim volume he was holding and said, "That was all you could find?"

"That was all I wanted," he corrected. "How about if I take yours out to the truck before we go any farther?"

Gina glanced at his cast and then down at the heavy box.

The book stall's owner caught her glance, as well as the quick frown on Nick's face. "Carryout service to your car is included in the cost of the books," the man hurriedly said.

"Ryan," he yelled and a husky-looking teenage boy

came hurrying over from the stall serving lunch. "Take this box out to the truck for these folks."

"Sure, Dad." Ryan crammed the rest of his doughnut in his mouth, grabbed the box as if it weighed nothing and headed toward the door.

"I'd better go unlock the truck for him," Nick said as he followed him.

"I'll look at the booths a little farther down," Gina called after him.

With a final smile for the bookstall owner, Gina moved into the armory. Within minutes her attention was caught by a display filled with both fleece and yarns from a local sheep farm. Fascinated, Gina watched as a woman spun the carded wool into yarn.

"Why doesn't she just go to the store and buy yarn?" Gina turned at the sound of Nick's voice.

"This is much more…" Gina gestured ineffectively.

"Work?" Nick supplied.

"Natural," she corrected. "I wish I could do that."

"We sell the natural fleece as well as all the equipment you need to spin it," the woman said.

But she wouldn't be here to use it. The thought depressed Gina. She'd be back in Illinois far away from Nick. Grimly she pushed the knowledge away, refusing to dwell on anything which would ruin the pleasure of the time she did have with him.

"I don't really have time to do it now," Gina finally said.

"We'll be here if you should change your mind," the woman said. "Just take one of our business cards. It gives the hours we're open."

"Thanks." Gina pocketed one before turning away.

Nick followed as Gina headed deeper into the stalls.

"Oh, how cute." Gina paused in front of a display of dollhouses.

"Elaborate toys," Nick said.

Gina leaned closer to one of the glass cases and blinked when she saw the price tag on a tiny set of china. "Not toys," she corrected. "That dinnerware set costs $462."

Nick studied it for a long moment and then said, "Why?"

"It's a hand-painted copy of a set used at Versailles by Marie Antoinette," the man behind the counter told them. "Miniaturists tend to prefer authenticity. For example, look at this house." He pointed out a large Victorian mansion to his right. "Try turning the light switch."

Gina gently flicked the switch, and the house lit up.

"Lights!" she exclaimed.

"That isn't all. Turn on the kitchen tap."

Gina did and was rewarded by a trickle of water.

"How do they do that?" she asked the man.

"There're batteries for the electricity, and the water recycles."

Nick watched the pleasure lighting up Gina's face and felt an urge to take up making dollhouses with her. It would be something they could do together, and it certainly interested her. And someday, if he could pull it off, they might have a little girl with Gina's soft silky hair or a boy with her bright eyes to play with it. He picked up the man's business card and pocketed it.

But first he had to somehow get Gina to stay within reach so he could convince her that marriage to him was a great idea. But how could he do that? He worried the question around in his mind as he watched Gina admiring the china bathroom fixtures in the dollhouse.

He'd never had the slightest urge to ask a woman to marry him before. He'd been too afraid a wife would come between him and his work. But Gina was different. Gina would understand that sometimes he had to put his work first. She wasn't a woman who would want to live her life through a man. She wouldn't demand that he spend all his time dancing attendance on her. She had outside interests of her own.

He smiled as he remembered the pleasure he'd felt last night at simply sitting in the living room with her, while she'd read a book and he'd studied the case notes on a heart transplant patient that a colleague wanted his opinion on.

Gina was that very rare person, someone who was willing to compromise on emotional issues. He watched tenderly as she smiled at the tiny cat in the dollhouse's kitchen. And because he loved her he was not just willing to cut back on his work schedule, he was eager to do it. Eager to spend all the time with her he could.

But did she feel the same? The question chipped away at his composure. She seemed to like him. She seemed to enjoy spending time with him. She seemed to like kissing him. But she'd given him absolutely no sign that her feelings went any deeper than warm friendship.

He wished the information about Boston College's teaching program would arrive so that he could start his campaign to convince her to transfer to Boston.

"Isn't this fascinating?" Gina turned to him.

"Fascinating," he repeated, watching the way her eyes glowed.

"Maybe you could..." She paused as she suddenly remembered his broken arm. Creating miniatures would probably take a lot of manual dexterity, and right now he didn't have any. This was hardly a hobby for Nick.

"Sorry, I wasn't thinking," she muttered.

"No, I can't do it now," he said, and for once he didn't feel the accompanying flash of pain at the thought. "But I get the cast off in a few more weeks. Maybe then."

Gina felt a surge of pleasure at the way he referred to the future. As if she were an integral part of his.

"Let's go see what else we can find."

Three hours later they finally quit after having examined virtually every exhibit.

"Did you see anything that appealed to the collector in you?" Gina asked as they left the building.

"No. I don't think there is a collector in me."

"Ah, well. It was a long shot," Gina said as she climbed into the truck. "Collecting tends to be passive, anyway."

"Passive nothing! Did you see the way that man at the comic book stall elbowed his way to the front?" Nick started the truck. "He probably lifts weights and studies karate to get ready for an event like this," he added.

Gina chuckled. "I will admit that some people seem to take their collecting more seriously than is good for them. Or than is good for the people around them."

"Do you want to stop somewhere for an early dinner?" Nick asked once he'd maneuvered out of the packed parking lot.

Gina briefly weighed the trouble of fixing something herself against the pleasure of eating alone with Nick and opted for home.

"I've already got some meat thawed," she said. "It won't take me long to fix it."

"Okay." He turned toward home with a feeling of pleasurable anticipation.

Thirty minutes later, he pulled into his driveway to find a strange car parked there. His gaze narrowed as he studied it. Could some man have finally shown up looking for Gina? He'd always found it unbelievable that she was unattached.

"It looks like you have company," she said.

Nick shot her a quick glance, but she merely looked curious. As if the strange car had nothing to do with her.

"I don't recognize the car." He cut the engine in the truck.

"Do you know all the cars in town?" she asked.

"Pretty much," he said.

"Maybe someone from Boston came to see you."

"Possibly," he murmured, looking around. "But in that case, where are they? I locked up before we left. You stay here," he ordered.

Getting out of the truck, he headed toward the front door.

Gina hurriedly scrambled out and ran after him. She wasn't going to allow him to face a possible intruder on his own.

"It can't be someone up to no good," she said, trying to reassure herself as much as Nick. "Otherwise they wouldn't have left the car in the driveway for anyone to see."

Nick frowned in exasperation at her. "Will you at least stay behind me till we find out what we're dealing with?"

"Women walking behind their men went out with the bustle," she muttered, but to Nick's relief she did stay back.

Nick paused as he unlocked the front door and pushed the door open. The hallway was empty. He looked at

Gina, who shrugged as if disclaiming any knowledge of where the person who owned the car was.

Gesturing her to stay where she was, Nick cautiously moved forward.

Gina nervously watched him approach the entrance to the living room. She didn't really think there was anyone hiding in the house, but there was that car out on the driveway and…

"It's about time someone showed up."

The woman's slightly peevish tones sent a shaft of horror through Gina. She closed her eyes and swallowed convulsively. You're imagining things, she tried to tell herself. Her mother couldn't be here. She purposefully hadn't given her the address. But she had told the lawyer. The memory made her feel faintly nauseated. She'd given him her address so he could send her a check. That was before she'd discovered that her mother was going to contest the will.

"Gina?" Nick's voice came from inside the living room. She'd been so caught up in her own fears she hadn't even seen him move.

Forcing her shaky legs to carry her, Gina walked through the hall into the living room. She could actually feel her skin blanch as shock drained the blood from her face. A buzzing sound echoed in her ears, reminding her that she wasn't breathing, and she hastily gulped in some air.

"Gina, darling. Aren't you going to say hello, after I came all this way to find you?"

Gina stared at her mother's petite body lying on the couch. Her forearm was lying across her forehead in what Gina recognized as her "brave, sick woman forcing herself to make an effort that was costing her dearly" role.

"How did you get here?" Gina's voice sounded tinny in her own ears.

Nick watched, curious about Gina's reaction. She wasn't happy to see the woman, whoever she was. In fact, Gina looked positively haunted. But why? he wondered.

His gaze swung back to the woman. She clearly wasn't a physical threat, but just as clearly Gina saw her as a threat of some kind.

"I had to fly, and it was such a trial," the woman's voice hardened slightly. "And then I had to drive from the airport to here. Thank heavens I won't have to do it again."

"Why?" Gina asked slowly. "Is someone coming for you?"

The woman gave a gurgle of laughter that sounded both artificial and calculating to Nick's experienced ear.

"Don't tease, darling," she said. "You'll be driving back, of course. It was very naughty of you not to send me your address. Fortunately, Mr. Mowbry gave it to me."

"I am not going anywhere with you," Gina said flatly, refusing to look at Nick. She knew what he must be thinking.

"Of course you are, dear," her mother said complacently. "I need you."

Her mother gave Nick a trembling smile. "I'm in very bad health. My heart, you know. I really do need her. And since Mr. Mowbry said she was only helping you with the housekeeping, you surely won't mind her going."

"I'm not going anywhere with you." Gina's face felt stiff with the effort it took not to burst into tears.

How could she ever explain her seeming heartlessness to Nick?

"How could you be so unfeeling!" Her mother dissolved into easy tears. "I won't be here much longer and then you can do exactly as you please. Oh..." She pressed her hand to her chest and gasped. "I feel so..."

Nick tore his eyes away from Gina's rigid features and, suppressing an overpowering urge to take her in his arms, decided to get to the bottom of this first. Gina was one of the most caring people he knew. Even the profession she'd chosen was one of helping kids. He didn't believe for a minute that she would abandon anyone who really needed her. He'd find out how this woman had gotten into his house later.

"Gina!" he said sharply, trying to yank her out of the frozen state she appeared to be trapped in. "Go upstairs and get my stethoscope. It's in the top right-hand drawer of the desk in my study. But first, would you introduce me?"

"Oh, I'm Helen Tessereck, Gina's mother," the woman spoke up. "I'm not surprised that you couldn't see the resemblance. Poor Gina took after her father. He was a beanpole, too, but what is acceptable in a man..." She grimaced expressively.

Gina practically ran from the room to get Nick's stethoscope. Even though she had no intention of going anywhere with her mother, she couldn't stay here now with Nick any longer. It was all ruined. Their friendship...their growing sense of companionship... All of it was shattered.

She shoved her hand against her mouth, pushing back the pained cry that tried to escape. Nick would think she was some kind of unfeeling monster for deserting her mother. He'd never want her to stay now.

She paused in the doorway of his study and took a deep, steadying breath. It didn't matter, she tried to tell herself. She still had her teaching. At least, she would once she finally received her legacy. Her shoulders felt bowed with the weight of her problems.

Trying to keep her mind on one thing at a time, she found the stethoscope and went back downstairs. She handed it to Nick, being very careful not to look at him. She couldn't bear to see the contempt that must be in his eyes.

"Why do you have that?" Her mother eyed the stethoscope he was holding.

Nick didn't answer her. He picked up her hand and, putting his finger on her pulse point, stared at the broad sweep of his watch's second hand.

"What are you doing?" her mother demanded.

"Trying to figure out why you should feel faint. Your pulse is steady and very good for a woman your age."

"My age!" Her mother jerked up, and then sank back against the sofa pillows as if suddenly remembering her chosen role.

"Gina, please help your mother sit up. I want to listen to her heart."

"I have no intention of allowing some man—" Helen began indignantly.

"Mother, this is Dr. Balfour. He's a thoracic surgeon associated with the Harvard School of Medicine."

"I don't care who he says he is. I have no intention of allowing a strange man to touch me."

Nick studied her petulant features for a long moment and then said, "As you wish. However, I can't ignore the fact that you claim to be having heart problems. What is the name of your family doctor?"

"I have no—"

"Dr. Whitney," Gina said. "I have his phone number in the address book in my purse."

"Please get it," Nick told her.

"No, I refuse to allow you to call him." Her mother looked furious. "There's nothing he can do from Illinois."

"He can fax your medical history to the hospital here," Nick said.

"I am not going to a hospital! I will see my own doctor once Gina and I get home."

"I am not going anywhere with you," Gina kept repeating the words in the hope that somehow they'd finally get through to her mother.

"We will discuss this privately back at my motel." Her mother shook off Nick's hand and got to her feet.

"I am not going anywhere with you," Gina repeated doggedly. "Not now, not ever." Unable to look at Nick, she blindly rushed out of the room.

Gina paused in the middle of the kitchen, her eyes blurred with tears at the thought of what Nick must be thinking of her. She didn't care what her mother's doctor or her minister or the lawyer thought, but Nick... She bit her lower lip to hold back the sobs. He wouldn't want anything to do with her after this. Even if she tried to tell him the truth about her mother, she couldn't prove it. Her mother's behavior was so far outside of normal as to be unbelievable.

She might as well pack her things and leave and save him the trouble of telling her to go. She gulped back the tears clogging her throat. At least her traveler's checks had been replaced. She did have cash again. Enough to rent a car and a room somewhere while she looked for a job and waited for her car to be replaced.

Taking a step toward her room, she paused when

something crunched under her feet. Looking down, she discovered she was standing on shards of glass. She sniffed, wiped her eyes to clear her vision and looked at the back door. One of the panes had been broken. So that was how her mother had gotten in, she realized. It was typical of her to simply destroy what stood in her way.

Not wanting to leave the mess, Gina started to sweep it up.

"What are you doing?" Nick's deep voice cut through her fog of misery, and she jerked, spilling the shattered glass she had been sweeping up back onto the floor.

"Cleaning this up. I'll pay for a new panel of course."

"Forget it. I'll find something to cover it with later. You know, I find it hard to believe that that woman is your mother."

Gina winced. "Everyone says that," she muttered. "Is there a taxi service in Vinton?" she asked, not wanting to have to ask him to drive her back into town.

"She doesn't need a taxi. She has a car."

"I am not leaving with her," Gina's voice rose with the strength of desperation. She had the scary feeling that if she got into that car with her mother, she'd never escape again.

Nick frowned. "Why would you? You don't really believe that there's anything wrong with her heart, do you?"

"What do you mean?" Gina looked at him uncertainly.

"I mean it's obvious that your mother is a manipulator. She uses her health to try to control the people around her, in this case you. She was what you were running from, wasn't she?" Nick suddenly realized, feeling an enormous sense of relief that there wasn't a man in Gina's background that he was going to have to compete with.

"Yes." Gina sighed. "I found out a few weeks ago that there was nothing wrong with her when her doctor accused me of trying to stifle her."

Nick gave in to his need to touch her and pulled her up against his broad chest. He wanted to erase the bleak, beaten expression from her face. "So you packed your bags and took off?"

Gina gave a watery chuckle, finding it impossible to stay miserable with his arms around her. "I didn't get very far, did I?"

"Your location feels perfect to me." He nestled his face into her hair, breathing in the light floral fragrance that clung to her.

"What's she doing out there?" Gina asked.

"She isn't out there. I told her either to leave immediately or I would call an ambulance to take her to the hospital."

Gina leaned her head back and stared up into his gleaming eyes. "And she actually went?" she whispered.

"And I doubt she'll be back. I told her that if she did, I'd call her doctor and tell him about her behavior here."

Gina gulped, unable to believe that he had seen through her mother's act. No one ever had before.

"So that takes care of your problem with your mother," Nick said.

"Only her physical presence," she said dispiritedly. "She's the one contesting my father's bequest to me. If I can't get her to change her mind by January, I won't be able to pay my school fees."

Nick glanced down into her pale face and felt a surge

of love swamp him. For a brief moment he considered asking her to marry him and phrasing his proposal as a mutually beneficial deal. He'd pay her fees, and she could... He swallowed at the directions his thoughts had taken. Much as he craved making love to her, he didn't want to if she didn't feel the same way. He couldn't bear it if she only tolerated his lovemaking out of gratitude.

And the only way to find out how she really felt would be to tell her the truth. The whole truth about his feelings.

Nick took a deep breath, steeling himself for the effort. If she turned him down... A blackness seemed to nibble at the edge of his consciousness, but he forced it back. He had to know.

"Marry me and finish your degree in Boston," he blurted out, and then winced at the bald sound of his words.

He felt Gina tense in his arms as if she doubted what she'd heard. He didn't blame her, he thought in self-disgust. Of all the clumsy proposals...

"Marry you?" she repeated incredulously. "But why?"

"Because I love you to distraction." He flung the words at her and held his breath, afraid of her response. If she turned him down...he didn't know how he would handle it. He could cope with having to give up surgery if Gina were there for him. But if she turned him down and left, he had the appalling feeling that his life would be a gray wasteland that not even regaining the use of his arm would dispel.

Nick bit his lip hard enough to draw blood, when he realized she was crying. Briefly he closed his eyes, desperately struggling for composure. Somehow he was going to have to convince her that... That what? he wondered. That her refusal wasn't going to destroy him. Yes, he told himself. He couldn't make her feel guilty simply because she didn't return his love.

"Don't cry," he muttered. "It isn't that bad."

"I'm not…I don't…" She chewed her lower lip uncertainly. "You wouldn't be saying that because you feel sorry for me?" she finally managed to voice her fear.

"Hell, no!" he said emphatically. "There are lots of ways to help someone without marrying them. If that was all I felt for you, I'd lend you the money you need and let you repay it when you finally did get your bequest. I want to marry you because I love you. I want to spend every night of my life making love to you. I want to come home from work and tell you about my days and listen to what your students have been up to. I want to have children with you."

Gina's body shook with the force of the happiness coursing through her. Nick really did love her. Not only that, but he was willing to share her with her pupils.

"Oh, Nick, I love you with all my heart."

His lips met hers, and a feeling of rightness engulfed her. This was what she had been born for. For this man and this moment.

Epilogue

"Dadadada!" Edward's high-pitched voice rose above the thumping of his chubby knees as he crawled across the hallway toward the opening front door.

His brother hurried after him, impatient to voice his complaint to his father. "Dad, teacher says I have to be a king in the Christmas play, but she hasn't got any camels for me to lead so I don't wanna." Max scowled at the thought of such poor planning.

Nick dropped his briefcase inside the door, automatically scooped up his youngest son and enveloped Max in a quick, loving hug.

"Sorry, sport, but being old enough for kindergarten means you have certain responsibilities, and taking part in the Christmas play is one of them. Camels or no camels."

Nick instinctively glanced over Edward's dark curls looking for Gina. His whole body seemed to tense when he saw her standing just inside the door to the kitchen. His gaze ran over her slender figure, lingering on her slightly swollen abdomen. Love and lust poured through him in equal amounts.

"Good evening, wife." Satisfaction filled him at being able to say the words. A satisfaction that not even ten years of marriage had dimmed. If possible he loved her more than he had the day he'd married her. "How are you and our daughter doing?"

Gina grinned at him and patted her rounded abdomen. "She's behaving herself for a change. Things were a breeze at school this morning, and this afternoon the boys and I went to the story hour at the library."

"It was great!" Max enthused. "The lady reading the story brought a big bird with her with sharp claws and a beak."

"A snowy owl," Gina translated.

"Me!" Edward suddenly planted a wet kiss on Nick's cheek and then tried to stick his finger in his father's eye.

"No." Nick jerked back. "We don't operate with our fingers, Edward."

Nick set Edward down on the floor and walked over to take Gina in his arms. She snuggled up against him, breathing in the crisp winter air that still clung to him.

"Dad, I really don't wanna be a king," Max insisted.

"And I really want to be alone with you," Nick whispered in Gina's ear.

Gina shivered longingly and planted a lingering kiss on his neck. "Later," she promised. "How was your day?"

"Hectic, and it was capped off by emergency surgery on some fool who not only ran a stop sign but couldn't be bothered to wear his seat belt. When he hit the other car, he was thrown against the steering wheel and crushed his chest. That's why I'm so late. It took me almost four hours to piece him back together, but I'm pretty sure he'll do.''

Gina gave him a proud smile. ''Of course he'll do. He had the best surgeon in the state of Massachusetts operating on him.''

Gina felt her heart swell at Nick's look of pleasure at her words. Sometimes she felt so happy she was almost afraid. As if she were tempting fate. She had everything she had ever wanted and a few things she hadn't even dared hope for: a loving, passionate husband; two precious sons; and in the spring, their family would be completed with the birth of their daughter. And she had been lucky enough to find a part-time job as a reading specialist with the local school district. Even her mother had finally been persuaded to seek psychiatric help. Her life was perfect, she thought, a second before Nick's lips met hers, and then she ceased to think at all.

*   *   *   *   *

If you enjoyed what you just read,
then we've got an offer you can't resist!

Take 2 bestselling
love stories FREE!

Plus get a FREE surprise gift!

Clip this page and mail it to Silhouette Reader Service

IN U.S.A.	**IN CANADA**
3010 Walden Ave.	P.O. Box 609
P.O. Box 1867	Fort Erie, Ontario
Buffalo, N.Y. 14240-1867	L2A 5X3

YES! Please send me 2 free Silhouette Romance® novels and my free surprise gift. After receiving them, if I don't wish to receive anymore, I can return the shipping statement marked cancel. If I don't cancel, I will receive 6 brand-new novels every month, before they're available in stores! In the U.S.A., bill me at the bargain price of $21.34 per shipment plus 25¢ shipping and handling per book and applicable sales tax, if any*. In Canada, bill me at the bargain price of $24.68 plus 25¢ shipping and handling per book and applicable taxes**. That's the complete price and a savings of at least 10% off the cover prices—what a great deal! I understand that accepting the 2 free books and gift places me under no obligation ever to buy any books. I can always return a shipment and cancel at any time. Even if I never buy another book from Silhouette, the 2 free books and gift are mine to keep forever.

209 SDN DU9H
309 SDN DU9J

Name	(PLEASE PRINT)	
Address	Apt.#	
City	State/Prov.	Zip/Postal Code

* Terms and prices subject to change without notice. Sales tax applicable in N.Y.
** Canadian residents will be charged applicable provincial taxes and GST.
  All orders subject to approval. Offer limited to one per household and not valid to
  current Silhouette Romance® subscribers.
  ® are registered trademarks of Harlequin Books S.A., used under license.

SROM03   ©1998 Harlequin Enterprises Limited

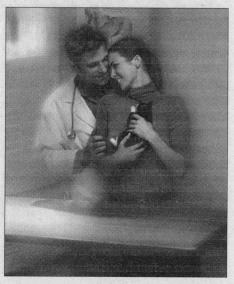

Through the shadowlands and beyond...

Three women stand united against an encroaching
evil. Each is driven by a personal destiny, yet they
share a fierce sense of love, justice and
determination to protect what is theirs.
Will the spirit and strength of these women
be enough to turn back the tide of evil?

On sale May 25.
Visit your local bookseller.

COMING NEXT MONTH

#1722 THE BLACK KNIGHT'S BRIDE—
Myrna Mackenzie
The Brides of Red Rose
Susanna Wright figured a town without men was just the place
for a love-wary single mom to start over, but then she ended up
on former bad boy Brady Malone's doorstep. Despite the fact
that Brady's defenses rivaled a medieval knight's armor, he
agreed to help the delicate damsel in distress. Now she planned
to help this handsome recluse out of his shell—and into her
arms!

#1723 BECAUSE OF BABY—Donna Clayton
Soulmates
Once upon a time there was a sexy widower whose precious
two-year-old daughter simply wouldn't quiet down. Suddenly
a beautiful woman named Fern appeared, but while she calmed
his cranky child, she sent *his* heart racing! Paul Roland knew it
would take something more magical than a pixie-like nanny to
bring romance into his life. But magic didn't exist…did it?

#1724 THE DADDY'S PROMISE—Shirley Jump
Anita Ricardo wanted a family but Mr. Right was nowhere
to be found—enter the Do-It-Yourself Sperm Bank. But
the pregnant self-starter's happily-ever-after wasn't working
out—her house was falling apart, her money was gone and
Luke Dole was turning up everywhere! She agreed to tutor
the handsome widower's rebellious daughter, but *Luke* was
the one teaching her Chemistry 101….

#1725 MAKE ME A MATCH—Alice Sharpe
When Lora Gifford decided to sidetrack her matchmaking
mother and grandmother by hooking them up with loves of
their own, she never counted on infuriating, heart-stopping,
sexy-as-sin veterinarian Jon Woods sidetracking her from her
mission. Plan B: Use kisses, caresses—*any means possible!*—
to get the stubborn vet to make his temporary stay permanent.

SRCNM0504